Praise for Kate Concealed

"I gave this a 5 stars because I started with the plan to read a few chapters before dinner and didn't put it down until early the next morning."
–Elizabeth, reviewer

"Couldn't put it down. Loved the storyline, the intrigue, suspense, romance, mystery. It needs to be a movie. Loved it!!! "
-J.B., reviewer

"The book was intriguing and it pulled you right in from the beginning. I was hooked. It was full of suspense and twists! I cannot wait for the third book to come out. I want to know how Kate's story continues!"
–Christina Tarbet, Reviewer

"Full of drama, great settings, choices and mysteries. It is also a clean read YA. – I like Cindy's writing style, her characters. I hated to have to put the book down." -Reviewer

"All I can say is WOW! This is an amazing rush of a book. Excitement, intrigue, twists and turns all surrounding one determined young lady. I love that this teen is decisive and determined to find out the answers and solutions. Great book, with strong characters."
-Teri Hicks, Reviewer

CODE OF SILENCE BOOK: TWO

KATE
CONCEALED

CINDY M. HOGAN

Also by Cindy M. Hogan

Audio, Print, and eBook

Watched Trilogy:
Watched
Protected
Created

Christy Spy Novels: Spin off of the Watched trilogy
Adrenaline Rush
Hotwire
Fatal Exchange

Code of Silence trilogy
Kate Unmasked
Kate Concealed
Kate Unleashed

The Royal Guard
Dangerous Truth
The Descension

Gravediggers

Sweet and Sour Kisses:
First Kiss
Stolen Kiss
Rebound Kiss
Rejected Kiss
Dream Kiss

CODE OF SILENCE BOOK: TWO

KATE
CONCEALED

CINDY M. HOGAN

O'NEAL PUBLISHING

For those seeking truth

1

Kate stared at the picture of her birth mother, Carmela, with the red X written over her face, the tell-tale sign a hit had been placed on her mom and she was believed to be dead. Kate refused to believe it. The crisp, almost new search journal cracked as she turned the page to look at a picture of her birth father, Vinny, holding her hand and walking her when she was a baby. She brought the fingers of her right hand to her lips and then down onto the picture. The ritual had begun two months ago after finding her birth father in New Jersey. She flipped back to the eerie picture of Carmela and whispered, "I won't forget you, Mom."

She shut the notebook turned journal and tucked it into the large box on top of her old, distended search journal, the one she'd used to catalogue everything she had found as she had searched for Vinny. "It's not the right time to find you. The leads have dried up. Sorry, Mom. One day I will find you, though." She said it with determination, her jaw set and her body rigid.

She grabbed her painting from the easel set up in her room and put it into her leather portfolio, the early morning sun erasing all the shadows of the night. After zipping it closed, she scooped up her duffle bag before exiting her room. Kate arrived a full half-hour early at Ellie's so they wouldn't be late. Ellie had a terrible time getting up in the morning and Kate knew that if she was awake, she was most likely still busy painting, finessing the project that was due in less than an hour.

She rapped three times on the Lamberts' front door before going inside. She passed Colby, Ellie's brother, who was dressed in his soccer uniform. He doubled back and gave her a quick hug. "Hey, Kate. Sorry, I'm late. Talk to you later." Without those reality TV shows he and Ellie had been obsessed with most of their lives, his focus had turned sharply on his two loves, soccer and research, Ellie's to painting. Even so, both Ellie and Colby's heads still jerked to the TV when it was time for a show they really liked. It was a work in progress.

Kate ambled into Ellie's room to find her standing in front of one of two easels, a paintbrush in her hand, her eyes fixed on the canvas. "Oh, Ellie," Kate said. "Tell me you finished yesterday and that isn't a wet painting we have to travel a half hour with to school." Ellie's eyes flicked to Kate and she gasped, stepping in front of the painting as Kate made her way around to look at it. "You started a new one?"

"Don't look, Kate, it's a surprise," Ellie said, her voice rising in pitch as she waved her hands up and down and all around to block Kate's view. But Kate had already seen the painting, in pieces, between Ellie's waving arms.

Kate stood like a petrified redwood tree. She ignored the echo of her pounding heart in her throbbing temples. The painting looked exactly like the picture of baby Kate being held by her birth mother that currently sat in the locket around her neck. The memories associated with it, not so great. She couldn't help but absorb every last detail of Ellie's painting as she forced herself not to shut her eyes against the despair that welled up inside her. The painting sent her sailing through an enormous rollercoaster of emotions from complete awe, peace, and relaxation to horror coupled with terror and dread. "This is incredible, Ellie. You have found your calling in life." The words scratched and clawed their way out. At last, Kate ripped her eyes away. Ellie's phone sat open, the screen filled with the picture inside Kate's locket. Ellie must have been using that as a reference. Kate's stomach still roiled and yet, now that she wasn't looking, a calm, peaceful feeling washed over her. The picture *was* beautiful. She hid the pain that screwed into her gut and smiled. "Were you up all night painting it?"

"You know me." Ellie smiled and rocked on her feet.

"Yeah. I still don't get why you have to do the things you love with such excessive fervor. You were the same way with those reality TV shows and now that you don't have them, you've put all your energy into your painting. Don't get me wrong. I'm happy you're doing something more productive, but seriously, it's okay not to do it to the extreme. Just 'cause you like it doesn't mean you have to do it constantly."

Kate lifted her hand to touch the painting, an irrational part of her thought it might be very much like touching her birth mother in the flesh, but a shimmer on the paint told her it was not yet dry. Ellie really had been working on it right before Kate had entered. Kate concentrated on the painting before her. The vibrant colors and the strokes seemed to come alive, different parts popping out at her at different moments—in just the right order somehow. A desperate longing for her birth mother erupted inside her.

The two girls were in the same painting class, but they were miles apart in skill.

"Well, I got stuck on this one," Ellie said, pointing to a familiar painting sitting on an easel to her right. She stood there, her lips pressed out in her thinking kissy face, the paintbrush still in her hand. She stabbed her brush toward the canvas without hitting it. "I can't get that color right. It's off, and it's driving me crazy." She pointed to a small section of the pear in the fruit bowl the entire class had been assigned to paint by today's class. Not only did the pear look perfect, but every piece of fruit appeared real, like Kate could reach out and grab it, just like with the other painting of her birth mother. She felt a bit sick inside thinking of her painting and how completely amateur it was.

Ellie shifted her gaze to the picture of Kate's mother. "I thought I'd get a head start on your birthday present. Now it won't be a surprise." She gave an exaggerated frown. "I needed a distraction." Ellie stared

3

hard at the painting.

Kate nodded toward the painting of Kate and her mother. "You did all this last night? Amazing." Kate stared at the picture, a whole new set of emotions flooding over her. It was her turn to wish for a distraction. She needed to get out of there. The thought of having such a likeness of her mother before her and not being able to reach out and hug her was killing her. Kate fingered the locket that held the picture Ellie was improving upon.

"Well, it's not done yet. You walked in before I could hide it."

"Really? It's incredible already." And I have no idea what problem you have with that one." Kate pointed to the fruit bowl. The smile that crossed Ellie's tan face was enormous and made her look even more gorgeous than she already was. She bit on the end of her paintbrush and a curtain of her blonde hair fell over her cheek. "Maybe I need to step away for a little while longer."

Kate pulled her own painting out of her leather portfolio. "Not even," Kate said. She took one look at it and then at Ellie's version and snorted before turning it around for Ellie to see. Ellie chuckled and Kate did too. Despite her best efforts, Kate's paintings always turned out looking like something a third grader would throw together.

Ellie reached out and took Kate by the arm. "It's cool in an abstract kind of a way."

"I'll take that. Now that I've made you feel better, pack up your *awful* bowl of fruit and let's go." Kate couldn't stop her eyes from flicking back to the painting of her birth mother. Her mother's chin rested on the top of Kate's head, gentle and loving. "You made my birth mother look just like me."

"You do look just like her. Your deep dark eyes, your almost black hair, and how your lips curve." Ellie shoved her painting into her portfolio. She must have noticed the longing on Kate's face because she followed that up with, "And you will find her. I know it."

"It's been over two months since Jersey and nothing. No leads." Kate zipped her portfolio closed.

4

"I know, but it took over two years for something to break with Vinny, and I know it didn't turn out like you hoped, but at least you found him. You know who your birth dad is now. Still no nightmares?"

"No. Nightmare free. You're right. Do you really think Carmela's alive?"

"Yes. You are and you were supposed to be dead. It's the same with her. She is alive, I know it."

Kate didn't look at her, but at the picture Ellie had painted. How was it possible for someone to put such emotion into a painting? The love exuding out of it hit Kate hard in the heart. "I can't search anymore. And, I really need someone on the ground in Jersey to work for me if I want to find her."

"You mean a PI? You don't have a good track record with them." She gave Kate the eye.

"I know. I don't have the money for one anyway." Ellie had been referring to the fact that Kate's parents had hired a PI using Kate's money, to keep Kate away from her birth parents. "It hurts too much, you know?" Kate didn't tell Ellie how she'd put her birth mother's search journal away.

"I know. But, I know you too and despite what you say, you'll never be able to give up. Not really. You'll find Carmela. There's no rush. Let things fall into place as they come—a nice gradual unveiling. I bet if you don't force it, the universe will send you what you need and want."

"What if I find her and it's not good news? What if she doesn't want me, or she's a bad apple?"

"You'll deal with that the same way you dealt with finding Vinny. It'll all work out, you'll see. We better get going, though. When I'm finished with these babies," Ellie indicated her paintings, "they will be perfect."

Kate stared at the picture of her birth mother for few more seconds and wondered how Ellie could change it to make it any more impactful and lovely, then followed her out of her room, convinced it couldn't be done.

Despite the underlying fear and sadness Kate experienced with the painting, a warm, comforting feeling filled her. One day she'd find her birth mother. She had to.

***

As they climbed out of the car at the university, Ellie said, "Oh, I almost forgot. Colby wants to take us to lunch today ... to talk."

"Hmm. It must be something bad then," Kate said, the last depressive feelings leaving her.

"Maybe, but he was smiling when he asked. He's up to something, and I think he thinks we will love whatever it is."

"Cool. I'm game." Colby was the big brother Kate would never have and she loved hanging with him. She had to constantly keep her childhood crush on him at bay. He was her best friend's brother after all. He had graduated and was getting ready to go to college. She and Ellie would follow him next year.

"He must've done something bad. Really bad. He's taking us to LaShays." Ellie gave Kate a meaningful look.

"That's one expensive restaurant. You think he destroyed something else?" Kate pulled her portfolio out from the backseat.

"Nothing could be worse than what he did with our dolls." She clutched her portfolio in her right hand.

"Your mom was able to get the hair replaced. I'm okay with it now. That was so long ago." They entered the college art building.

"Yeah, now you're okay with it, but when he came to us and told us he'd accidentally chemically burned all the hair off their heads, you cried for days." Instead of coloring the doll's hair, his chemical had disintegrated it.

"Yeah, but that was years ago." Kate frowned, rubbing her neck.

"Try three."

"It was my favorite doll. And I don't remember you handling it all that well, either."

"That's what I'm saying. I can't imagine what horrible experiment he's decided to include us in. Why do I have to have a mad scientist

6

brother anyway?" They reached the second floor and started down the hall to the art studio.

"You have to admit it comes in handy. Especially when we have science projects and assignments."

"Yeah, but not great when he destroys everything with his experiments."

Kate laughed as she opened the door to class. "I agree with you. But if this meeting with him gets me awesome food, I'm there."

"Thank the lucky stars we didn't let him try the chemical on us."

"And why we didn't make him try it on himself first, I'll never know." Kate rolled her eyes.

"Oh, and he'll take me home so you can go straight to your kung fu class." She snorted. "I can't believe you almost have a six pack already. You'll be a female Thor before I know it."

"Very funny. Ha. Ha." Pride rose up in Kate, but she played it off, quickly putting her painting next to all the others that were waiting to be graded.

Class flew by while they tried various painting techniques that Kate was barely able to do or couldn't do at all, while Ellie excelled and finally got her color right. She should really have been in a more advanced class, but she refused to move up, saying she still needed to get a firm grip on the basics. Kate knew she only said that so Kate wouldn't be left alone. And it was her luck or Kate's that the same teacher taught all levels and was willing to make accommodations for Ellie. So, while the rest of the class struggled, she conquered, creating masterpieces while Kate's mind returned over and over again to the painting of her birth mother and the journal she'd tucked away in her closet.

2

Ellie and Kate laughed at a cat video on Ellie's phone as they waited for Colby to show up at LaShays restaurant. His car pulled up five minutes late. "What's so funny?" he asked as he gave his keys to the valet.

"Check this out," Ellie said, showing him the video.

They laughed again as the short clip played. "Who videos this stuff?"

"Thanks for taking us to lunch." Kate gave him a friendly smile.

"What did you do?" Ellie gave him a sidelong glance.

"Hey, can't a brother take his favorite girls out to lunch just because?" He put his arms around their shoulders, sandwiching himself in-between as he led them inside.

"No."

They all chuckled. The hostess led them straight to their table where Colby deftly changed the subject from one thing to another until their food came.

"Okay, master of distraction, lay it on us. Why are we here?" Ellie asked, taking a bite of her green beans.

"Well, I've hit a snag with next week." He glanced up at each of them in turn before taking a sip of his drink.

"What?" Ellie said, leaning toward her brother, her face screwed up in question.

He held up his hands.

"I know I told you two that I'd take you camping this next week, but it's not going to be possible. I'm going to have to flake on you." He whipped his hand through his unkempt brownish blond hair somehow making it look even sexier than before.

"What?" Ellie shot back. "I thought you just ruined something of ours. This is much worse."

"Yeah. That's definitely worse than you ruining our stuff." Kate huffed.

"I'm sorry, but I'm going to be in Italy." He held back a grin.

"What?" Ellie screamed. "You got in?"

"Yep." He let the grin fill his face. "Someone dropped out of the science program. He got totally sick or something. So, I'm in. I'm heading to Bologna University."

"The first alternate wins. Sucka. Take me with you." Ellie bounced on her seat.

"That's the thing. You guys could come." His eyes glinted with merriment.

"Oh my gosh. We could?" Both Ellie and Kate squished their bodies close to the table, leaning toward him.

"I mean wait a week or something, but yeah." He took a bite of his salmon.

"We have our painting class. We can't miss it. We only have next week off," Ellie complained.

"I understand that, but you might have to make a sacrifice."

"Mom's not going to let us miss one of our last weeks of class. No way. We'll have to go next week."

"I'll be settling in." He gave Ellie the stink eye.

"Fine, we won't come the first day. When do you go?" Ellie was a freight train. They'd be going next week for sure. If Kate's parents allowed it.

11

"Sunday night and I get there on Monday morning."

"Then we'll come Wednesday." She patted her hands on the table like all had been decided.

"Thursday." Colby pressed his lips together.

"Fine. We'll come Thursday." She squealed. "Looks like we get to go to Italy after all." She bumped shoulders with Kate.

"Yep." Colby set his glass down. "That will be good, because if you leave here Thursday, then you'll get there Friday and be there for the weekend."

"Then we'd have to miss class on Monday then. No. We'll arrive Wednesday." Ellie set her jaw. "We need at least four full days there."

Colby scoffed.

"We'll be jetlagged and all that stuff the first day. You won't even notice us."

"Alright, arrive on Wednesday, but be warned, I've heard the accommodations are Spartan."

Ellie waved her hand in the air. "Ah, it's Italy."

"Like you've been," he said, teasing her.

"No, I've heard and I don't care." She turned to Kate. "Now we have to convince your parents." It was like she could read Kate's mind.

"Yeah, I guess saying I'm in one place and going to another is out." Her insides squirmed thinking about how she'd told her parents last spring that she was going to Mexico with Ellie's family when in truth she went with them to New Jersey to find her birth parents. It hadn't ended well.

"Let's not repeat that little adventure," Colby said, his eyes sad, but resolute.

"I bet they'll let you." Ellie grinned. "It's only a couple of days."

"You think? I'll also have to find the money. I spent it all in Jersey, remember?" She slouched in her seat.

Ellie rolled her eyes. "No, your parents spent it all on that fake PI, trying to keep you from your birth parents. In truth, they owe you. By the way, I'm glad you stopped calling them by their first names. That was weird."

"Yeah. It was weird for me, too, but I thought I was making a point. Taking a stand that they couldn't lie to me or I wouldn't consider them my parents." Kate didn't want to do anything to rock the boat at home right now. When she had come back from New Jersey and had her talk with her adoptive parents, they had been so relieved to see her. They had worried buckets over her. She'd forgiven them and didn't want anything to get in the way of their relationship again. Maybe there was another solution. "Okay. I'll ask them, but they won't like me being away."

"You were going to be away anyway."

Kate nodded, sitting up straighter. "You're right. Okay. I'll ask." It would work out. It had to.

***

Ellie had taken the self-defense class with Kate for a good month, but opted out when Kate said she wanted to keep it up and take it every day. It made her feel powerful somehow and she was glad her parents had forced her to take it in the first place. After only a few weeks of the class, her nightmares had become less frequent and eventually, had totally stopped. The first few weeks at home, Kate could hardly go outside without thinking the Marconis would find her. FBI Special Agent Johansen had reminded her that she was relatively safe for two reasons: The first was the fact that while the mafia guys had seen Kate was flying to Dallas from New Jersey, they had no idea she lived two hours away from the airport. The second was that they didn't know her last name. Without those two things, he assured her, they would not be able to find her. Kate was too common a name in Texas.

Kate grabbed her duffle from the backseat and hurried inside to change into her workout gear. She was totally excited to be sparing with Jake today. She looked down the row of students and easily spotted his tall, bulky frame. Her heart raced thinking of ways to overpower him, but first they had to do warm-ups. Her newly muscled legs and arms stretched and contracted as she went through the practiced movements. It seemed her muscles had lengthened since she'd started running every morning three weeks ago. She'd never felt better.

Everyone split up, moving to their section of mats to spar with their assigned opponent.

"You ready for all of this?" Jake said, his gloved hands indicating his muscled body.

"I was wondering the same thing," Kate said, grinning as she slipped protective padding on her legs and hands.

He chuckled and said, "Don't worry. I'll go easy on you."

That was the last thing Kate wanted. If a Marconi or Bellini goon ever found her, she needed to be ready and Jake was built like one of them. If she could disable Jake, she knew she'd be ready for them. "You'll be sorry if you do."

He chuckled, but after they bowed to each other, she let loose on him, her speed and agility working to her advantage. She danced around him, getting in a jab here and a punch there for several minutes. He swung and kicked, but she moved out of his way before there could be any contact, until there was. His right cross connected with her chin and she went down. It was a solid, powerful hit. He lunged toward her, prepared to finish the job. But she wasn't going to let that happen. She rolled, shaking her head slightly to get rid of the ache in her jaw. He landed hard on the mat on his hands and knees, missing her only by a second. She pounced on him, one arm around his neck and the other swiping his arms out from under him. His face hit the mat with a thud. She whipped her legs around his, immobilizing them, and pinned his arms under him. He struggled, but couldn't move. She had done it. When he relaxed, she did too. They got to their feet, both breathing hard, and bowed to each other. She had done it. He put his hand on her shoulder and said, "Good job. I hate losing, but that was good."

"Thanks," she said as their instructor came over to join them.

"Good fighting, you two," then he went on to give them advice about the fight and what to work on next. Sweat dripped down between her breasts and down her back as she listened, a sense of euphoria hitting her. If she had to, she could face a Marconi or Bellini and actually have a chance. She worked still harder for the rest of the class, taking instruction and insisting that her body perform to its maximum.

As she drove home, she thought about Colby and sparring with him again. He would like the new moves she had learned. She had been practicing some moves with him when he had a spare minute here or there. His strong soccer legs kept her on her toes, and it was fun to teach him stuff and watch him progress. She realized that her previous sparring session with him would probably be her last, though. After he went to Italy, he would be heading off to school in New York. The thought twisted inside her gut and made her tired, but thoughts of Italy dashed them away. She needed to ask her parents.

3

"Mom. Dad. I have exciting news." Kate's parents sat stiffly across from her on the sofa, smiles plastered on their faces. Her dad's dark eyebrows shot up in question. "Remember that study abroad science program that Colby applied for?"

They nodded.

"He got in."

"Good for him. What does this have to do with us?" Her dad seemed relieved her announcement hadn't been more serious.

"Yes," her mom said. "Why the whole, *let's go talk in the living room*? This is something you could have told us anywhere."

"Well, you know how he was taking us camping next week? Well, he's leaving for Italy on Sunday and can't take us anymore." She could have ended there and led up to the Italy thing, but she felt it best to treat the situation like she was ripping off a Band-Aid and do it fast and clean. "But he wants us to come and visit him." She set her elbows on her knees and cradled her chin to stop her hands from shaking.

Her mom's blue eyes widened for a fraction of a second. Her dad's hand landed on her mom's knee and squeezed.

"I don't know. What about your art class and your self-defense classes?" her dad asked after clearing his throat. "I'm not excited about throwing all that money away."

She sat up. "There's no school next week. We'll go on Tuesday night and be back Sunday night. We won't miss anything. And it's not like you were expecting me to be here. We were supposed to be camping all week. You'll have me an extra two days all to yourselves. I'll be safe. And this isn't like last time. We're truly going to Italy." She smiled and tried to slow her slamming heart. She wanted to address all the possible objections at once.

Her dad leaned forward. She was sure it was in an attempt to seem relaxed, but there was something about his movements that seemed stiff. He looked anything but relaxed. Her mom's face paled. They couldn't think she'd go behind their backs again. "Seriously. I learned my lesson. No more sneaking around. You can trust me."

Her mom's lips turned up into a slight smile, but it was her dad who spoke. "We are trying to, honey, but there are other concerns too, like money and supervision and where exactly you'll be."

"We'll be at the University of Bologna. The oldest university in the world. That alone should make you want me to go."

Her mom did seem to relax, her shoulders rounding slightly, her stiff posture leaving her.

"And, I was thinking, it's a good way for you to pay me back for the PI." A zing of fear whipped through her at saying something so bold when her parents could easily say no and completely end her chances of going to Italy, but she tried to say it in a nonchalant way, so as to seem normal and right.

Red climbed up her dad's neck and her mom's cheeks were suddenly blotchy. Not a good sign.

"The only costs will be food and airfare. We can stay in the house Colby is staying in. We'll be with him the whole time. You trusted him to take us camping."

"What about his program? Won't he be in classes or something?" Her dad still didn't look convinced.

Kate knew Colby would be in class a majority of the time, so she chose to deflect the question. "It's only really four days. Tuesday and Sunday will be travel days. Please. You've got to let me go. I'm sorry for springing it on you, but Colby only found out yesterday."

"As for the money, we were going to put it back into your savings account." Shame laced her dad's words.

"Yes, and I can do with it what I please, right?" She sucked in her lips. She hadn't meant to say that out loud. Her nerves were making her reckless.

"For school."

"There will still be some left. Besides, hello, oldest University in the world? Another country? Educational opportunities abound." She flung her hands around in the air, desperation setting in.

Her dad looked at her mom, raising his eyebrows. She didn't say anything. It must have been more than she could bear to let Kate go without them again.

"Come on, Mom. Please. I know what you're thinking. The original Bellinis may have come from Italy, but that was forever ago. My dad and all his crazy mafia relatives are in New Jersey. I'll be clear across the Atlantic. If I survived Jersey with them, I can definitely survive Italy without them."

Her mom gave an almost imperceptible nod.

Her dad frowned but then nodded as well, narrowing his eyes at her mom for the briefest of moments before turning to Kate. "I guess that's an okay."

Kate stood up and hugged them. "Thank you for trusting me. You won't regret it."

"Make sure we don't," her dad said.

She kissed them both on their cheeks and rushed out of the living room and up the stairs. Then she remembered she needed to tell them to get with Ellie's mom to arrange the flight and headed back. She slowed as she heard her parents' loud, intense whispers. She stopped to listen.

"What was I supposed to say? If I said no, she'd just go running there anyway 'cause she'd know we wanted to keep something from her." Her mom's voice was totally exasperated.

"She couldn't go without us allowing it."

"After what happened this spring and New Jersey? She's smart. Resourceful. And almost eighteen."

"Well, maybe you should tell her."

"No. There's no need. We don't want her to have any reason to go searching while she's there. She's better off not knowing."

"But—" her dad started to say.

"No!" Her mom's voice was harsh, firm. "Not happening." Then she said something Kate couldn't understand. "It's far away from there anyway. She'll be fine. She's going for fun this time. Let's allow her some fun. We both know that didn't happen in Jersey."

"But she's going to be in Italy. You must see the problem here."

"I don't. She was right. The Bellinis and Marconis who know her are all in New Jersey."

"We told her no more secrets."

"No more secrets that involve her. This doesn't."

Kate thought about just barging in and making them tell her—no secret was a good secret. Then she took a step and the floor squeaked. The whispers went silent. Startled, she carefully backed away down the hall and up the stairs, grabbing a few things to make herself look busy in case her parents decided to come check on her. Moments later, her dad walked in.

"Hi, sweetie." He looked around as if by doing so he'd be able to ascertain how long Kate had been in the room. "We were wondering if we needed to do anything to uh, you know, book your flight and all." He'd obviously not thought of an excuse on his way up there.

Kate worked hard to keep her voice even. "Oh, yeah. Just give Mrs. Lambert a call. She'll make the reservations and everything. She has some lady who works for them and gets them awesome deals. And Dad, thanks again for letting me go to Italy. I know you guys are worried about me traveling with the Lamberts because of Jersey, but you don't need to be. I'll be safe and there's nothing for me to hunt down in Italy.

And so you know, I've stopped actively searching for my birth mother. There are no leads and if there were any they'd be in Jersey." She was speed talking without realizing it.

He stepped toward her. "I know, sweetie. We trust you. Just remember that your mom is still a bit fragile from what happened in Jersey. I know you would end up going with or without my permission sooner or later, and since your mom doesn't object, neither do I. You've seen what can happen when you don't follow our advice. All we want to do is keep you safe."

A shudder rushed through her as she thought about being imprisoned by the Bellinis. "Keeping me from Italy is not going to keep me safe."

"I realize that. Please honor this one thing—call us daily. Email. Send pictures. I know Special Agent Johansen has been watching the airport and stuff, but remember that people are still looking for you."

"I know, but it's been three weeks since any Marconi or Bellini goons landed anywhere in Texas. Johansen said he thinks they've given up on searching for me right now. And, I will call every day. I promise."

"I'm sure he's right," he said and cleared his throat. "And I'm glad you've given up your search." He pressed his lips into a smile. "I'm sure it wasn't easy to make that decision."

"Thanks for trusting me. I know it scares you."

"Yes. It does, but we are working on that."

Kate nodded. "And, I'm really sorry about New Jersey, Dad."

"You don't need to continue to apologize for that. It's over and done. No more living in the past. Life is for the living. Live, Kate."

"I intend to, Dad. Thanks." He often had such words of wisdom. And he was right, she hadn't been living, she'd been buried in the past.

"We'll pay for your plane ticket. Everything else is on you. You'll have to use some of that PI money we're putting back into your savings."

"Really? The plane ticket won't come out of my money? And you're paying me back?"

He smiled. "Yep!" It seemed a weight lifted from his shoulders and that he grew several inches.

"Thank you!" She popped off the bed and gave him a big hug. His strong arms surrounded her and lifted her a couple inches off the ground for a few seconds.

"We've seen some real positive changes in you since you got back from Jersey and we want to support that. I can't believe you will officially be an adult in less than two months."

"I can't believe it either." He let her down and she took a step back. "This time next year I'll be getting ready to leave for college."

"Don't remind me. Oh, and promise me you'll stay with Colby and Ellie and not go anywhere on your own. "

"No worries there, Dad. I wouldn't want to."

"Good. And if you discover anything you don't understand while there, know you can always talk to us about it."

"Okay. What might I find?" Her heart pounded.

"I don't know," he said, shrugging his shoulders acting like it was nothing. "Italy is not anything like the U.S. and if you discover you have questions, know we are here for you." He smiled.

If she nudged him a bit, maybe he would tell her what he really thought she might find. She might learn about the secret. She opened her mouth to speak, but then he said, "Are you still going to the beach with the Lamberts tomorrow or does Colby need that time to get ready?"

The trip to the beach had been planned a good month ago. The Lamberts' last family outing before Colby left for school. "Yep. Colby said he'll have plenty of time to do what he needs to today to be ready for his early flight on Sunday."

Her dad snickered and leaned on the door casing.

"What?"

"Okay." He grinned from ear to ear.

"What?"

"He's a guy, but I guess he could be ready." He shrugged.

"It is Colby, though." She laughed. "And, I'm sure Ellie will help him."

21

He raised one eyebrow and left.

She squealed and grabbed her phone to tell Ellie Italy was a go, ignoring the little twinge she felt rush up her spine.

***

Kate woke drenched in sweat, her throat dry and scratchy. It had been weeks since she'd had any nightmares. Tonight, the dreams had returned. It had to be because of all the talk about her birth mother, the mafia, traveling, and Ellie's painting. That haunting painting. The painting that made her ache to be in her birth mother's arms. She shook her head, trying to get the images of Carmela being shot in the head out of her mind. While her subconscious had superimposed Carmela's face on the woman, it didn't mean it was in fact her.

Her dad's words played in her mind. *Life is for the living. Live, Kate.*

She pushed the memories and dreams to the side and got up. She needed to shower and then she'd feel better. She was going to Galveston with the Lamberts and she was determined to have a good time. She wouldn't let a silly dream change that. Life was meant to be enjoyed, and she had spent the last two years living in the past, in pain, and it had to stop. It stopped now.

Even though it was early on a Saturday, Kate's mom stood at the stove and her dad sat at the table waiting for her, like every morning. The one thing that was different was that her sisters and twin brothers wouldn't be joining them before she left. During the week there was school and on Sundays was church, so Saturday was the only day they were allowed to sleep in. But her parents never slept in if someone was going to be awake.

"Morning, sweetie."

"Morning." Kate sat at the table and her mom brought her two pieces of egg in the basket. They were crunchy and buttery, just how Kate liked them. "Thanks, Mom. This is delicious." She drank her orange juice and swallowed her vitamins.

"I'm glad you like it. You better hurry, though. Don't you need to be at the Lamberts' at six-thirty?"

Kate glanced at the clock. She had two minutes. "Yep." She ran her plate to the sink and then brushed her teeth in the bathroom before grabbing her beach bag and heading for the door. Her mom and dad met her there, her mom holding out a large paper sack. "I made peanut butter cookies and put some apples and bananas in here for everyone. Make sure you say thank you to the Lamberts."

"I will. Love you, Mom and Dad. And thanks for the goodies. Later." She took the bag, rushed out the door and hurried two doors down to meet up with the Lamberts.

4

Kate and Ellie sat in the very back of the SUV and Colby sat on one of the middle captain chairs while their parents drove and sat shotgun. Pop rock played through the speakers and Ellie's mom was singing along.

Colby turned in his seat and faced the girls. He looked tired, and so did Ellie for that matter. Kate felt a little run over too. She had woken three times with nightmares, only two that she could remember clearly. "So, I know why I'm beat," Colby said. "And I know why Ellie has bags the size of Kansas under her eyes, but you, Kate, why do look like you didn't get any sleep?" Ellie had already told Kate she'd been up all night helping Colby pack. Kate's dad had been right.

"You don't want to know."

Ellie grabbed Kate's arm. "Are you having nightmares again?" Kate looked at her hands. Flashes of being chased by the mafia and having her house burned down flickered across her mind. She couldn't hide it.

"Why?" Ellie's mouth fell open, and her incredulous stare bored into Kate.

Kate knew she wouldn't be able to keep it from them even though she wanted to. "I don't know. Maybe it's all the talk about Jersey and traveling and stuff." She was sure that pulling the box with the two search journals down this morning and going through each page of both hadn't helped the situation. In her defense, she had put them back and at that very moment they were sitting hidden in the box at the top of her closet.

"Oh, I'm sorry. The painting, too?" Ellie covered her mouth.

"No. No. I love that." She did love it, but at the same time it made her feel terrible. It had definitely contributed, but no way would she let Ellie know that.

"But it's making you upset, obviously." Ellie shoved herself deeper into the bench.

"No. It's not. Really." Maybe if she said it enough, it would be true.

"That sucks, Kate." Colby said. "I wish I could climb into your brain and get rid of all that terror."

A blush rushed into her cheeks. It was when Colby said stuff like that and looked so freaking sincere, that Kate's heart swelled with admiration and love for him. "Thanks. I wish you could too."

"Agent Johansen is still monitoring the flights into DFW, right?" Colby put his hand on Kate's knee.

"As far as I know. It's been almost a month since I've talked to him." She realized he would probably want to know that she was leaving town for a few days. She'd call him later.

"I think no news is good news." Ellie opened her eyes wide and nodded.

"I agree." Colby leaned back in his chair and grinned at his sister. "I won't mention why Ellie was up all night." He huffed.

Kate nudged Ellie. "Wait! I thought you were up helping Colby."

"Only until two," Colby said. "At three I found her with a paintbrush in her hand."

"Ellie. Moderation. Remember?"

"I had to finish it. I knew I wouldn't be able to work on it today."

"Did you finish it?" Kate hoped her face only showed excitement.

Ellie lifted her chin and exposed her neck before giving a crisp nod. "I did."

"It's really amazing," Colby said. "Life-like."

Kate gulped.

Ellie's satisfaction turned on a dime when she looked at Kate's expression. "I thought I was doing something nice for you, but it turned out to be something bad."

Kate obviously hadn't been able to hide her unease. "No. Please. Who knows why I'm having those dreams again. It's not your fault. I really do love it."

"Well, you're not going to get to see it until your birthday. Don't even ask."

"I guess Italy wasn't super great timing." Colby frowned. "Combined with that painting, it probably sent your subconscious reeling."

"Why would it do that?" Kate pushed into the seat and huffed. "I wear this locket every day. The same picture is inside."

"Hello, you're Italian." He said it like that answered every question.

Kate held back what she was going to say, suddenly realizing that she was Italian, or at least her ancestors were. "But what does that have to do with anything?"

"You're going to Italy. Your whole soul is excited about it. Think about it. Somehow your body and mind know they're about to be with the very people who are your people. You'll be able to see what it is that makes an Italian—you—tick."

"I have no idea what you're talking about." Kate peered out the window, watching the barren landscape go by.

He sighed. "By going to Italy, you are getting the chance to uncover and explore your Italian-ness."

"I'm American," Kate said. "Just like you and Ellie."

"You've learned to be American, but in truth you are Italian at your core. Your parents and their parents and their parents' parents are all Italian. That makes you Italian too." He gave a short, curt nod.

"That's crazy talk." She kept her eyes fixed on the landscape out the window.

"No, it isn't. It's the truth. Studies have been made that prove that who you are is determined almost solely on genetic make-up." Colby's voice was completely level as he spoke. He totally believed what he was saying. "You simply aren't aware of it. It's going to be cool in Italy because I'll be able to see and help with some of the continuing research on this very thing."

"Careful, Kate," Ellie said. "You're stepping into his scientific world."

"Shut up, Ellie." He narrowed his eyes at his sister. "This is cutting edge stuff."

Ellie only laughed and set her head on the pillow that was wedged up against the window.

"My parents were American." Kate wasn't about to buy what he was saying. "And we don't know anything about my birth mother's ancestry, let alone her parents'. Not even really about Vinny. He was most likely born in America too."

"Where you are born does not make you a native. Your birth parents are *Italians living in America.*"

"So you're trying to tell me that my adoptive parents have had no effect on me?" Kate scoffed. What he was saying seemed ridiculous.

"It may appear that they do on the surface, but deep down, you will end up behaving as your genes dictate. It's science." His determined stare seemed to look right into Kate, straight into her genes.

Kate thought about her birth father, her uncles, her grandfather— all in the mafia, all doing terrible things—and her head throbbed. The thought of having her actions dictated by their choices sent heat to her face. "Hold on, Colby. I don't care what your studies say. I'm not going to end up like my grandfather Salvatorio or Vinny. I would never choose to be a part of the mafia."

"I'm not saying you'd make that exact choice, but I am saying that you are Italian. You are a part of the Italian consciousness whether you like it or not. You may make a few choices that don't fit. They are outliers. If you were to study the Italian people and how the majority react to the same situations it would be very similar. It's a fact of life. Like I said, science. Just like Ellie and I make a lot of decisions based on our Englishness. It's not good or bad. It just is."

"I think your science is a bunch of gunk." Ellie stuck out her tongue, but her eyes remained closed.

"Kate, you're going to Italy. You may not be there long enough to see just how affected your decisions are by your Italian-ness, but hopefully, you will be able to see how similar you are in thinking and basic beliefs. It will be interesting for you."

"I don't know that I want to acknowledge it even if it is true." This was a strange concept to Kate. She had always felt her choices were her own. A few of her not-so-nice choices flitted through her mind.

"Come on. Get in touch with your heritage. Get to know who you really are. I think you might like what you find." He winked, hands clutched together. His sincerity was charming, but she wasn't buying it. Not yet.

"Maybe I don't want to be Italian. Maybe I just want to be what I am. An American."

"Scientific studies do not lie. Just sayin'." He leaned forward in his seat.

"Well, stop saying," Ellie huffed, eyes still closed.

Colby spun his chair around and said, "It's okay to explore your Italian roots, Kate. Don't be ashamed of who you are."

His words tumbled around Kate's mind. Scientific studies, seriously. It couldn't be true. It was really just the age-old question of nature vs. nurture. That would always be under debate. There would never be a true resolution of the question because it involved people and people were unpredictable. She wasn't ashamed of who she was. She was an American. She glared at the back of the seat Colby was sitting in and turned on her headphones to finish listening to an audiobook for the rest of the four hour drive. A light snore sounded from Ellie's direction. She was full-out. Kate wanted to tell her about the conversation between her parents she'd overheard, but it would have to wait.

***

A light breeze wrapped around Kate as she climbed out of the car and stretched. She'd fallen asleep at some point on the drive and finally felt rested. The full extent of the heat and mugginess that would claim the day hit her as they carried bags and equipment through the sand. She was glad she'd put her swimsuit on under her clothes and wouldn't have to seek out a bathroom.

As soon as they found their spot, equidistant from the two nearest groups, they all disrobed before setting up the umbrellas and chairs and laying out their towels. They raided the cooler and took long drags of their drinks when done. It was just after eleven and already sweltering.

"Last one in is a beached hippo," Colby called as he took off for the water. Everyone set their drinks down and charged after him. The water was warm. Almost too warm to be refreshing, but still felt better than the moist, hot air.

A couple hours in, they retreated to the shade of their large umbrellas for lunch. Kate eyed her towel, thinking she could get in a quick nap. Fighting waves was tiring. Then Ellie squealed, "Oh, my goodness. The boys here are so tantalicious. Let's go talk to those ones over there. The one with blond hair can't keep his eyes off you."

Kate chuckled at Ellie's new word, *tantalicious*. "Nice try. All the guys' eyes are only on one person—you. But, if you want to go talk to them, I'll come with you." With Ellie's long, tan legs, full blond hair, and blue eyes, guys couldn't help but fall for her immediately.

"You've got to at least give one of them a chance." Ellie's eyes were fixed on a group of six guys playing beach volleyball.

"I don't know." Kate bit her lip.

"Look. You need to forget about Duran."

Kate gave her friend a deadly look. They hadn't talked about Duran for several weeks. Every time they did, contention sparked between them.

"I don't mean forget, forget," Ellie backpedaled. "He's always going to be the boy who risked everything and saved you from the mafia, but you have to move on. You can't be with him. Ever."

"Why, Ellie? Why? Why can't we be together?" Memories of the pin Duran had given her to identify her to the FBI filled her mind. The FBI had secretly removed her from their office after a raid on the Marconis' club and reunited her with the Lamberts at the airport. Without that pin and Duran getting the FBI to save her, she'd still be in New Jersey, hidden away by the mafia and doing who knew what dirty work for them.

"He's in New Jersey, for one. Two, he's neck deep in the mafia: your father's family, I might add." Kate sighed. They'd been over this a thousand times, but it never got easier to understand.

"But, he helped me get out. Why can't he get out? Maybe we can do something."

"Kate. Come on. You know nothing can be done. We can't do a thing to help him. And I'm going to help you forget about him and those boys over there are going to help too. Get up. We are going to do some forgetting together." She stood up, held out her hand to Kate and smiled. Colby frowned at her. Kate huffed, but took the proffered hand and went.

The closer they got the more obvious it was that these were college boys. Ellie had a gift for finding and seducing all guys, but older guys were her specialty. Ellie could easily pass for college age, but Kate never felt she could. It made her feel uncomfortable, like the little sister that tagged along with her hot older sister because her mom made her. However, it made Ellie happy, so she did her best to exude college-age-ness as they sat in the sand near the court and watched. Ellie picked out a couple guys and instructed Kate to cheer for them. Exactly what she wanted to do.

It didn't take long for the guys to notice them and give them appreciative nods for the cheers and encouragement, but that was as far as it got. After the third game, it was obvious the guys were there for some serious play and getting with a couple of girls, to Kate's relief, was not on the agenda. At least not today. The girls found themselves in the water again, floating and swimming and splashing while the sun continued its relentless assault on them, making it hard to find any relief from the heat.

Ellie and Kate sat and watched Colby and his dad toss a football back and forth, occasionally throwing themselves into the waves to snag a diving catch. Ellie's mom sat on a floaty in the water. "So, are you going to embrace your Italian-ness?" Ellie waggled her eyebrows at Kate, obviously mocking Colby and his science.

Kate gave her a dirty look. It'd become a sore spot, something that nagged at her.

"Whoa, that was one terrible look. I'm not saying I agree with Colby. I fell asleep somewhere during your very interesting and provocative conversation, but I do think you should explore your heritage and see what your life could have been like had you been born and raised in Italy. You may never get that chance again. What if you go with the attitude of learning about the Italian people and the *what if* of your life? Instead of being tourists, we could immerse ourselves as Italians. It would be fun."

"I don't know if I could do that. I've never thought of myself as an Italian."

Ellie's forehead wrinkled. "Really? But your birth parents..."

"What I mean is, I've always just considered myself an American, born and raised. I've never entertained the thought that I was anything else and I'm not sure I want to claim that possible part of me. Seriously. That part of my history is messed up. I don't want to identify with my mafia uncles and grandparents."

"But what about your birth mother?"

"What about her?"

"She was good, right? We've decided she turned good. Don't you want to claim that piece of Italy she's given you?"

Carmela hadn't even crossed her mind, but Ellie was right. Kate did think her birth mother was good. She couldn't reject her or that part of her heritage. She could try to explore what she thought or hoped was

31

good and leave the bad behind. It had to be possible. When Kate didn't answer right away, Ellie added, "I mean, she was an FBI agent, right? She was going to bring the bad guys down."

Kate smiled. She loved how Ellie wanted nothing more than to make her happy. "While I know Vinny and Salvatorio and my uncles and aunts are 'bad'," Kate used hand quotes, "I don't know that Carmela was. You're right. All the evidence points to the idea that she was good and wanted things to change. But, I don't know that I can explore what she had to offer me without touching the bad stuff too. And there's no evidence she was an agent. It's better that I leave this one alone at least for now. We should go to Italy as tourists. I've already ruined one of our trips. I'm not going to ruin this one too. Who knows what we'd find. If you want to pretend to be Italian some of the time, I'm totally game. But I'm American."

Ellie's big lips pushed out into her famous kissy-face, but she said nothing more.

However, Kate couldn't stop thinking about her Italian-ness. The idea of it stirred and bubbled in her gut. Then she realized she still hadn't told Ellie about the conversation she'd overheard.

"I think my parents are keeping something from me."

Ellie's eyebrows shot up. "Again? Seriously?"

"After I got them to let me go to Italy, I overheard them arguing about something, so naturally, I listened in." Ellie nodded, but frowned. "Anyway, it sounded like my dad didn't want me to go because of something I could find in Italy."

"That's weird. Italy's nowhere near New Jersey."

"I know. They said something about me being a curious enough person to go looking for whatever it is."

"Hmm. More intrigue in the Hamilton house. Why am I not surprised?"

"Yeah. I should have stormed in and forced them to tell me the secret, but I chickened out."

"Just confront them about it tomorrow. After church, you know, when they're in really good moods."

Kate chuckled. Ellie liked to believe that church always made everyone genial and open to agreement.

"I don't know. Maybe."

Colby's dad came back to their beach umbrellas with his wife and Colby waved the girls out. Some cute local guys joined their tossing game. It was a lot of fun, but Kate would never forget Duran. Never.

5

"I'm sorry I'm not going with you to the airport," Kate said early the next morning while she hugged Colby in the Lamberts' driveway. She hadn't been to an airport since she had returned from New Jersey and the thought of going to one brought terrible memories of Galtem, a Marconi goon, who had spotted her in the airport in New York when she had been trying to escape the mafia. He had tried to detain her, but in the end, he was captured and taken to jail.

"I get it. But, you're going to have to get over your fear or else it's going to be a bit hard to get to Italy." Colby leaned back and peered into her eyes. She tried to look away, but he pulled her back into a hug. "Besides, I'm not worried about you, not with you kicking my butt with your Kung Fu magic." He loved to tease her about her classes.

"It's not Kung Fu." Kate smirked.

He hugged her tighter. "I hate seeing you scared, that's all."

"Yeah. I thought I was over it."

"I think it's going to take more than self-defense classes to make you forget. I don't know how someone gets over being held captive and forced to do someone else's bidding."

Kate shivered as Colby pulled back. "I was pretty lucky my father was the one who kept me in Jersey. It could have been a lot worse."

"There you go, always choosing to see the positive in what most would find the most horrifying thing ever."

"I have to, otherwise I'd be a mess and I refuse to let them make me fear every moment." A deep ache sat in her gut. Kate clenched her stomach trying to get rid of it, but she knew it would stay until she talked to Special Agent Johansen. She should have called yesterday after she had those nightmares. For some reason, he always made her feel better.

"Well, I'll see you in a few days. Can't wait."

"Me, neither. Have fun."

"You know I will. Oh, and here's something you can chew on for the next few days. You'll never know how you fit in this world if you don't explore your past. Your heritage."

Kate crossed her eyes and stuck out her tongue.

Colby got into the car with the rest of his family including Ellie and they drove away as Kate waved. She headed home and went straight for the kitchen, dropping off her pillow and overnight bag at the base of the stairs. She heard her mom talking and slowed her gait, not wanting to interrupt. If her mom was talking to someone this early in the morning, it had to be something important. Kate quietly rounded the corner. Her mom was by herself and she wasn't on the phone, but she was talking to herself. And not in English. Kate froze and watched her mom for a minute, searching for a phone set on speaker on a counter. Her mom swung around, a big white cookbook in her hands. When she spotted Kate, it seemed that her mom's eyes froze in shock for a quick second, but she recovered quickly. "Kate. Good morning."

"Morning, Mom. Were you just speaking another language?" Kate furrowed her brow.

"No." Her mom smiled but didn't offer any explanation.

Kate narrowed her eyes and shifted on her feet.

"I mean, I'm trying. Yes. I've been using an online translator and stuff. We're having this Italian dish for lunch today. How was Colby?"

She was changing the subject and Kate knew it. "He was great. Totally excited to get to Italy. The program won't know what hit it."

Italian?

Her mom put the cookbook up in the cupboard and continued working at the stove. "I can imagine. I hope he'll work hard while there and not get caught up in all the new and exciting things to see and do."

Kate eyed the cupboard. She'd seen that book before, but had never really looked at it. "This is Colby we're talking about. Mr. Scientist. He applied for this program over a year ago and has been waiting anxiously ever since. I'm sure he won't squander the opportunity."

"I'm sure you're right. He is a good boy." She smacked her lips before pressing them into a flat line.

"Yes, he is." Kate hated it when her mom referred to someone as *good*. No one was purely good or evil. Her thoughts drifted to Vinny, her birth father. She had to believe he was more good than evil.

"You'd better go get ready for church. We leave in thirty. The kids have already eaten and are ready."

Kate wanted to ask her mom more about the Italian, but knew she'd barely have time to get ready as it was. She would ask about it later. She ran upstairs, took a quick shower, but didn't wash her hair. No time. She slipped on a skirt and blouse and pulled her hair into a messy bun and then looked at herself, Colby's parting words screaming at her. *You'll never know how you fit in this world if you don't explore your past. Your heritage.* Her olive skin, her shiny, dark brown hair, dark eyes, and something about her facial features told Kate she was Italian. Did that mean something in those same genes which defined her looks also defined her choices?

She still had a hard time swallowing the idea, but it was growing on her. A little seed had been planted and she was deciding if she wanted to pluck it out now or wait until she had some proof that it was ridiculous.

***

Kate listened intently to the sermon, not that she usually didn't, but she found questions rolling around in her brain as the priest spoke. Maybe she could ask him what he thought about genes and decisions. Certainly he would have answers. He had direct discussions with God.

Yes. She would ask him.

She waited patiently afterward for the regulars to finish their praise of his sermon and then she moved in. Her family had already left the building and she felt a bit anxious by how long it had taken.

"Why Kate, how are you doing?" Father Sebastian asked.

"I'm okay." She gave him a small smile.

"Good. Is there something you wanted?" He tilted his head slightly as he asked.

"Yeah. I was wondering if you could answer a few questions for me." Kate's heart thumped and she wrung her hands.

"Certainly." A few stragglers came and shook the priest's hand and thanked him for his thoughtful words.

"Well, I was wondering how in control we are of our own destiny. I mean, you said in your sermon that we must decide to follow Christ and stay on the path so that we can be saved, but someone the other day told me that we are predisposed to act and choose certain things. Does that mean that in reality we are a slave to our genes and have no real ability to choose?"

"Well, that's a pretty complicated question. Are you studying nature vs. nurture in school right now?"

"No. It was just something someone said to me. This guy was of the opinion that my choices, while I believe they are my own, are not and are in fact determined by the genes that I was born with."

"Well, there is some truth to what *that guy* said, but we are not animals. God gave us the story of the creation in Genesis so that we can understand this concept. We do have choices. Unfortunately, many of us are not strong enough or aware enough to realize we have made a decision not based on what we know, but on what we are predisposed to do because of our genes or upbringing."

"So I do have a choice? My ancestors don't determine my choices?"

"Yes, but to determine if your choice came from your own will or the will of a previous ancestor or parent, it's hard to say."

"So, I don't have a choice." Kate grimaced.

"That's not what I said. This is a complicated idea for you to be hashing out, and I'm afraid I don't have a simple answer for you. We are influenced by those who came before, but I firmly believe if we become aware of that influence, we can choose differently than they would."

"That's why this concept is constantly under debate."

"Yes. However, remember that you are not an animal and aren't run by your instincts. You have a large functioning brain that can override the base instincts you were born with. You can be in control."

"Okay." Her words came out hesitant, unsure.

"And Kate," he said. "You haven't come to see me about what happened in New Jersey in more than a month. Is everything still okay?"

She hesitated, but only for a second. "Yeah. Everything's great. Thanks." She hated lying, but her family had already been waiting a long time for her. She left feeling just as confused as she was before, but in a different way and with different ideas. Maybe she needed to explore her heritage in order to recognize where her decisions were coming from. Maybe by understanding her Italian-ness she'd be able to control her decisions. Maybe only her instincts were Italian. And she didn't have to listen to her instincts.

She examined the stained glass windows as she walked to the doors of the chapel and she thought about Jace and how he'd taken his own life in Jersey. Her heart ached at the memory. Genetics or free agency? Was it his genes that made him believe the world was better without him in it? But, then why had Kate chosen not to take her life when she discovered what she had about her parents? Why had she chosen to fight? Was it because of her heritage? Maybe Italians and more specifically, her line of Italians had a fighting spirit that didn't allow her to think the world would be better and instead needed her. At the moment she felt she was a puppet and the puppet master was her genes. She walked out into the sunshine, leaving the church and meeting up with her family who had waited for her outside.

"Is everything okay, sweetie," her dad asked, putting his arm around her. He smelled like he always did on Sundays, fresh and minty.

"I think so. I just had a question for Father Sebastian."

"I'm assuming he answered?"

She nodded. "Yep." She hated that she still felt so unsettled.

"Alright. Let's go get some lunch. Your mom cooked Italian."

Kate was glad her parents hadn't asked her about the question she'd asked the priest. They were good like that. Her stomach grumbled thinking about food. She'd only eaten a piece of toast at the Lamberts' before Colby left.

She was starving by the time they got home and went straight into the kitchen, but she was the only one. Everyone else had run to their rooms to change. Her eyes fell on the cabinet holding all the recipe books. She looked around and then headed quickly toward it. She flung open the cupboard and pulled out the book her mom had been looking at. *Il Talismano della Felicità.* She opened it and found lots of pictures, but also lots of words, all in Italian. No English included. The name Donati was scribbled on first page. She thought back on her mom holding the book in the kitchen earlier. Nowhere had she seen a phone. Her mom hadn't been translating anything. She knew Italian. What did that mean? Had she learned Italian in college? Had her parents spoken Italian to her as a child? Where had she gotten this book? An ache spread through Kate's gut. She heard the patter of bare feet heading down the hallway, and shoved the book back into the cupboard and shut the door. Then moved quickly toward the oven.

Her brothers raced in. "We're supposed to set the table!" They set the table with the dishes their mother had stacked on the table before church. When finished, they took a seat even though there wasn't any food on the table and no one was there to serve them, playing with their utensils as if they were wild animals.

The girls came in next, chatting about some event at their school next week. Closely behind were Kate's mom and dad. "Go ahead, Kate. You can pull it out of the oven. It should be ready." Hot pads in hand, Kate opened the oven and pulled out the pot. It smelled heavenly.

Her mom slid a drawer open and using a wooden spoon, stirred the vegetable mixture inside the pot, taking a quick taste. She then sprinkled a little salt onto the food before putting the vegetables into a big bowl and the Italian roast onto a platter. She pulled out some crusty bread from the cabinet and butter from the fridge.

Kate desperately wanted to ask her mom about the Italian she'd been speaking, but it didn't seem like the right time. She'd ask her after lunch.

***

Kate went to find her mom after doing the dishes and came upon angry whispers instead. Her parents were in their room, their double doors slightly ajar.

"No. We can't tell her now. I refuse to expose her to that," her mom hissed.

"But this is Kate we're talking about. She's suspicious. I think we should just get it all out there into the open."

Kate's feelings of betrayal rushed back as all the anomalies of the day flashed through her mind, heat spreading up her neck.

"No. She doesn't need to know. She's not going where it will affect her. Not really."

"She's going to be in Italy. It's not that big of a leap."

There was a pause before her dad continued.

"I know she isn't your biological child."

"Really, Tom? Really?"

"No. Hear me out."

Her mom said nothing. Kate wished she could see them.

"She looks like you in so many ways, everyone says it. Her birth parents are Italian. One day she is going to put it all together and realize the truth. And, if we aren't careful, she'll feel our tension and know something's up. We should face this head on."

"There's nothing to face. It's my secret. Not hers."

"What harm would it do to tell her?" Exasperation filled his words.

"This isn't about her this time, Tom. It's about me."

"But it involves her."

"It doesn't. It's my past and I want to keep her as far away from it as possible."

He huffed.

So, it was her mom's secret? What secret could her perfect mom be keeping from her and what did it have to do with Italy? Kate wanted to barge in and parrot what her dad was saying, but she didn't want to miss anything and she didn't want her parents to clam up when she stormed in. No, she'd listen and when they were done spilling all their secrets, she would join them and tell them she knew and the drama would be over.

"Like I said the other day, this doesn't affect her. I never want her to know, and she doesn't need to know. She needs to have a good time and forget about her birth parents and all of that for a while. We don't need to be throwing anything else onto her plate."

Her mom drew in a ragged breath. She'd been crying. "I can't escape my past, but she never has to be involved in it. Why can't you understand this?" Sobs filled the air. "Why can't my past stay dead and buried?"

Kate felt a bit ashamed for listening in at that point. Her mom was allowed secrets. Her own secrets. Kate had to admit she had some of her own that she'd never share with her parents because they didn't have any bearing on them. Heat filled Kate's cheeks thinking about her mom knowing some of her secrets. Kate backed away deciding her mom's secret would remain just that, her secret. At least for now.

Kate joined her brothers and sisters in the family room and played games. After a while, their parents joined them. As the hours passed, the secret wedged itself between them. Kate couldn't seem to relax. So much for not caring. She needed to clear the air if she was going to be okay.

Finally, after the kids went to bed, Kate found her mom. She was watching a movie on TV with her dad.

"Mom. Dad."

They looked at her in question and muted the TV.

"Is there anything you think I should know? Are you keeping something from me? It feels like you are." She wanted not to care about her mom's secret. She'd give her mom one more chance to tell her.

Her parents looked at each other.

"Well," her mom said. "As a matter of fact there are things we keep from you."

Kate frowned. "But you said no more secrets."

"Yes. I did, but I guess what I meant was no more secrets between us. No more secrets that affected both you and us. We will always have secrets, because we are your father and mother, but we will never keep a secret from you that you should know."

"I guess I understand that, but I feel like you're keeping something big from me and I don't like that."

"We would let you know if we thought it affected you." Her mom's smile looked genuine. She really believed it. But her dad did not look so comfortable.

"So you'll tell me if I need to know then?" Kate rocked on her feet.

"Yes."

"I hope I can be the person who would be okay with that." She scrunched up her face.

"You are that person. We were thinking of going for a picnic at the park tomorrow. Good idea?"

Kate nodded. "That sounds great, actually." But, she had to get more answers. "What if I ask you a direct question about something? Will you be honest with me?"

They nodded, looking a bit nervous.

"Even if it's something you don't think I should know or question?"

"Of course."

Kate wanted to ask about the Italian, but chickened out. They'd made a lot of progress and she didn't want to send the relationship backwards. And, if she was being honest with herself, she wasn't sure she'd be able to handle what they told her.

"Okay. I'm going up to my room then."

"Night. We love you." They said it in unison and Kate knew they really did.

She hung back to see if they would say anything more. She couldn't help herself.

"I told you she'd sense it," her dad said.

"She is very intuitive. I wish we could catch a break with her, though. Why must danger be all around her all the time?"

"We should tell her. If we continue to hide it, she's going to start digging and make something out of it that it isn't."

"No. It's not about Kate directly. There's no reason for her to find out. I don't want to open any doors for her. I want to protect her. Let's let the past stay in the past."

"Fine," he sighed. "But for the record, I think it's a mistake."

"It'll have to be my mistake."

The movie started playing again and Kate made her way to her room, more curious than ever. The secret must be something awful for it to make her mom so upset. Did Kate really want to know? After hearing what she had, she knew she could never ask. Maybe she could find out her mom's secret without getting it directly from her. She wanted to be able to forget there was something she didn't know and accept that she didn't need to know everything, but if her mom was Italian and that was her secret, why was she keeping it from her and why had she left that life?

As if walking into her room and seeing her bed was the gateway to her memory, Kate realized she hadn't called Johansen. She looked at her phone. It was ten, which meant it was midnight for Johansen. She'd have to wait until tomorrow to call him. Kate opened her closet door and fished out her two search journals—again. She flipped through the one she'd finished at the beginning of summer, chronicling her search for her birth father, and set it on her desk. She looked at the other one, the one that was to chronicle her journey toward finding her birth mother. She stared at it, all the dead ends crashing into her. She opened to the first page and looked at the picture of Carmela. No, she thought. She was not ready to start up that search again. And even if she was, there was nothing to go off of. She'd explore her Italian heritage instead. And maybe look into her mom's secret just a little. She and Ellie would play Italian together and hopefully, it would make her a wiser choice-maker and let her know what she was up against.

6

The air was calm and the partly cloudy sky made their time at the park a dream. Not too hot and not too cold. Kate had left a message for Special Agent Johansen early that morning and kept looking at her phone, hoping to see a message or a missed call or something. At noon there was still nothing. As soon as the watermelon, sandwiches and chips were gone, Kate's siblings ran for the playground, even Jori and Amelia. Her dad followed behind, ready to play. Kate and her mom tidied up, repacking everything into the cooler and the picnic basket. Kate kept glancing up at her mom. People did always comment on how they looked alike, but Kate could only see the blaring differences. Her mom's milky white skin under her jacket, the light freckles across her nose and her blue eyes. Since she didn't have any family for them to visit, Kate had never really asked about her mom's family.

"Mom," she asked, taking a seat after closing the cooler. Her mom shut the picnic basket and said, "Yeah?"

"What were your parents like?"

Her mom went rigid, her body still bent over the basket. Then she came to herself, though her speech seemed rehearsed and it appeared that she had to really think to remember what to say.

"I had a beautiful childhood. We lived on a farm, well, more like a ranch. Lots of people were always about, ranch hands and workers ate almost every meal with us. They had their own bunk houses on the property, but most of them were men and didn't want the responsibility of cooking."

She stopped and smiled like she was done. Kate hated to press. She knew her grandparents had died when her mom was young and it was sure to bring up bad memories, but something inside her wouldn't let her back down. "I wish I could have seen the ranch and met my grandparents. What were they like? Did your mom look like you?" She wanted her mom to say where the ranch was located. That would answer a lot.

Her mom turned away and when she turned back, her eyes were filled with moisture. She nodded. Kate felt bad she'd pushed. She slid down the bench to her mom and hugged her. "Mom, I'm sorry, I didn't mean to make you sad."

Kate's mom nodded quickly a couple times and hugged her hard. "No matter how much time passes, it's still painful."

It took several moments before her mom released her hold on Kate. Kate figured she wouldn't get anything else out of her and was shocked when she spoke. "My mom was a vivacious woman. Full of life." Kate held very still listening. "People said we looked alike, yes, but I always thought she was much prettier than I was. She was adventurous and never backed down from a challenge. Your grandfather was much like your grandmother only with a dash of seriousness and firmness. He was a businessman at heart and loved to work just as hard as he liked to play. He sought out challenge. He had a never-die spirit for sure."

"They sound wonderful. What were their names?"

Her mom cleared her throat. Kate leaned forward, excited to learn their names and what that would tell her.

"Alessa and Piero."

Stetson and Jarem, Kate's seven-year-old twin brothers came barreling over to them. "Hurry up, you two. We're going to play tag. We need more people." They had dirty hands and a few bits of wood chips clung to their sneakers already.

"We'll be right there," their mom said, but the boys didn't leave; they pulled on Kate's and her mom's arms until they relented, her mom giving her a wink as they followed.

***

Kate cornered her mom a few times to discuss her past over the next two days, but somehow, her mom always found a way to get out of saying anything important. Kate could remember her mom showing her pictures of Kate's grandparents when she was younger, but couldn't remember what they looked like. Maybe if she could find the pictures, she would get some answers. She'd searched everywhere she could think of, even going through the boxes in the attic and looking behind all the panels. The only place left was her mom and dad's room, but she hadn't found a good time to search in there because someone was always around. At lunch on Wednesday, she discovered an opportunity.

"Why do we have to go, Mom?" Jori asked.

"It won't hurt you to spend a few hours helping others, will it?" The church sponsored a big silent auction every year that earned a ton of money to help the homeless.

"But, it's going to be boring," Jori whined.

"Everything can't be fun," her dad said. "But, don't you remember last year? You two had a great time." He indicated Amelia and Jori. "You had a great time because it feels great to help others."

"It was fun last year," Amelia said. "Remember, Jonathan was there and you two got to work together. I was with Sam. We packaged and labeled everything for the people who won."

"You think Jonathan will be there again this year?"

"Probably."

"I'm in, then."

"Good," their dad said, "but try to do it with a thankful heart and not one that is chasing a boy."

The girls giggled.

Kate took the chance. "Do you think it would be okay if I stayed behind to do some last minute research? I'm feeling a little stressed about leaving tonight."

Her mom sighed. "I think you should have used your time more wisely the past few days."

"Please."

"You'll be here all alone."

"I'm here alone a lot."

"Not all the time."

"Nothing will happen. Please."

Her mom shared a look with her dad and she said, "Fine, but next time do you think you could not wait until the last minute?"

"Yes."

"Please have everything down by the front door. We'll get back at three and will need to leave directly."

"Sure."

Kate helped with the dishes and her brothers and sisters hugged her goodbye. They would be going to an aunt's house on her dad's side after the auction so they wouldn't have to endure the long trip to and from the airport. After her family left, Kate went up to her room and pretended to research, just in case her parents came back for whatever reason. She decided she'd better text Johansen. Since she couldn't reach him to talk to him, she would leave him a text message.

Kate: *Just thought you should know I'm heading to Italy for the rest of the week. Colby is doing a study abroad at Bologna University and Ellie and I are visiting him. I'm kinda worried about you. Are you okay? It's never taken you longer than twenty-four hours to call me back. I hope everything is okay.*

Kate sent the text and waited. When no response came after about five minutes, she stalked her way to her parents' room like a cat burglar, startling at every sound. Her heart thumped hard in her chest and she felt cold as she entered the room. She stood there frozen for some time, fear of not only violating her parents' privacy, but also of what she might find, rooting her to the spot.

She reminded herself that all she wanted to do was find some pictures of her grandparents and mom when she was a child. There was nothing bad about that. She forced her body to cooperate and started a methodical search in one corner of the room. She worked fast, moving furniture and shuffling through the contents of everything that held anything. She even climbed under the bed with a flashlight. No pictures. No documents. As she scooted back out, she noticed a bump under the rug. The bed was solid wood and without moving it, she couldn't get under the rug. It was securely pinned to the floor by the legs of the bed.

She rushed down to her dad's workshop and brought back a yard stick which she shoved under the rug and used it to nudge the bulge out. It was hard work, especially since she had to hurry. Her parents would be back in ten minutes and she hadn't brought her things down yet. What if the auction took less time than usual? They could come home early. She set her alarm for eight minutes, and jabbed, poked, and dragged the stick until finally, the items came free from their tomb.

Pictures. Black and white pictures. Kate's hands trembled as she picked up the first one. A man and a woman in their late twenties sat on a horse in a beautiful green field. The names Piero and Alessa were scrawled on the back of the picture in swirly script along with the word "Italy" and a date. Jackpot. She'd found pictures of her adoptive mom's mom and dad. Why they were hidden under the bed, she'd never understand. Piero and Alessa looked happy, peaceful. Kate took a picture of it with her phone, excited to see more. She set the first picture to the side and then picked up the next. Her hand flew to her mouth.

The people in the picture were dead, bodies splayed in odd positions with blood or bullet wounds visible. Horrified, she shuffled through the rest. All were similar. All with obviously dead people in them. Kate dropped the pictures and stifled a cry. Then for some reason, she looked through the pictures again, flipping them over and reading the names and dates on the backs and spreading them out in front of her. Only one picture had living people in it and it was the one with her grandparents. Why was her grandparents' picture mixed in with the ones of dead people? She leaned back against the footboard, looking at the pictures, but not focusing on them. The words she'd overheard her mom say played through her mind. *Why can't my past stay dead and buried? It's my past and I want to keep her as far away from it as possible.* Kate's eyes focused on the pictures again. Was that the past she was referring to? Were her grandparents murderers?

She heard the front door open downstairs. "Kate?"

Kate whipped around, scooping up all the pictures and then shoving them back under the bed, using the yardstick to push them deep under the rug. She heard the footsteps in the hall getting closer. She stood up in a flurry and moved toward a large dresser, not sure what to do next.

"Kate," her dad said. "What are you doing?"

She stared at a picture of her adoptive parents that sat on the dresser and reached out to pick it up. Hot fire licked her insides. Who were these people she lived with? If they didn't have anything to do with what happened in those pictures, why did they have them? "Don't worry, I'm ready." Her dry mouth couldn't get her tongue to work properly, and her words came out slow, even. "I just realized I didn't have a picture of you guys and thought I'd grab one to take with me."

"Oh, I don't think we have any current ones printed." Her dad walked toward their nightstand. "Let me see."

"It's okay." Her eyes darted toward the end of the bed where the yardstick stuck out a few inches. She stepped quickly toward it and tapped it casually with her foot until it disappeared under the bed. "I'll just take a picture of this one with my phone, and maybe get a candid at the airport."

"Good idea. Your stuff in your room still?"

"Uh-huh." Her dad left the room. A fog of confusion settled over Kate as she snapped a picture of her mom and dad from last year's family pictures.

"Let's go," her dad said from outside her bedroom door, clutching her large and small suitcases, her bag slung over his shoulder.

It was like she couldn't feel herself, like she wasn't real, like everything was happening in slow motion. She walked toward the door, her feet heavy like sledgehammers. Her dad was already halfway down the steps when she reached them. She wasn't sure she'd be able to walk down them. Maybe she shouldn't go to Italy. She needed to find out what those pictures were about. Her dad looked up at her from the bottom of the steps.

"Step on it, Kate. We need to go if you are going to make your flight."

Somehow, she got her feet to move down the stairs. Her dad didn't wait on her, but left through the front door. She walked out into the bright, hot sun, but couldn't stop the shiver that rushed through her as she spied her mom sitting in the front seat smiling out at her. Maybe the pictures had nothing to do with her mom's parents. Maybe she was overreacting. Her mom could not have come from parents who would murder people in cold blood. Kate needed to tell Ellie about it. She needed to have time to think. Italy could give that to her. Italy could give her the processing time she needed before confronting her mom about the pictures. About her past.

She willed her feet to move to the car and she slid into the back seat. She closed her eyes and tried to block everything out, including the images she'd just seen. No wonder her mom didn't want her to know her secrets if they included the fact that Kate's grandparents were murderers. And why did her dad think it would have been better for her to know? She wished she had never seen those pictures and never wondered if her grandparents were responsible for them.

7

Kate woke in the backseat of the car, interrupting the new nightmares of her adoptive mom shooting people, Kate's grandparents laughing as she did.

"Are you okay, sweetie?" her mom asked.

Kate brushed her hands over her face, the dream dissipating, but the adrenaline continuing to make her heart pump like a steam engine. "Just a nightmare."

"I thought those had stopped," her dad said, looking at her through the rearview mirror.

"They had, but I guess they're back," her voice was sour, resentful.

"Are you sure you're all right?" her dad asked.

"I'm fine," she huffed, squirming in her seat as she tried to find a more comfortable spot. "You know I'm Italian. Well, hopefully I'm going to discover what that means while I'm in Italy."

Her parents had shared a quick glance and then her dad, who was driving said, "What exactly does that mean?"

"Well, Colby seems to think that our genes have a lot to do with our choices, and I want to see if my choices have been markedly Italian or not. I want to see if I do stuff simply because my birth parents were Italian or if I've been choosing of my own free will. Or if you two have had any effect on my behavior."

"Interesting," her dad said. "But, I think you'll find you are the master of your destiny and not those who came before. Have you ever heard of such a thing, Abrie?"

Her mom gave her dad an exaggerated frown from the front passenger seat. "It sounds like a perverse take on nature vs. nurture to me. Kate, you have control over who you are and what choices you make."

Kate had thought about saying, *You mean like your parents had control over their decision to kill all those people?* but held back. She'd get nowhere doing that. Her grandparents were probably not even involved. Maybe she could do a little research while in Italy and find out if her mom was Italian and who her grandparents were if they had been involved with anything terrible. She stared at the back of her mom's head. A feeling of pity and then pride washed over her, surprising her. Abrie had turned out okay despite what Kate thought her grandparents had done. Even though her gut ached thinking about it, she was able to come to a conclusion. Her mom had escaped her genes through her choices, maybe Kate could too.

Her dad pulled up to the airport curb and helped her pull her luggage out of the car. Both her parents hugged her tight and her mom whispered, "Let us know when you land."

When Kate pulled back she said, "I will. No worries there." Her mom's phone vibrated and she pulled it out of her pocket. Kate saw a message pop up on the screen. Not in English. Italian. She quickly pocketed the device after a glance. Kate should have asked her right then and there what it was all about, but her dad said, "You're going to have to hurry, sweetie. We're a bit later than expected." Her mom's eyes filled with tears as Kate walked into the airport terminal. Kate forced herself to push the pictures to the back of her mind, but Ellie noticed something was wrong the second she saw Kate.

"What's wrong? You look pale." They hurried to the long security line.

"Nothing."

"Seriously? You're not getting sick or something are you?"

"Me, sick? No way. I think I just got a little carsick. Potato salad for dinner."

"Eww. Sorry. I've got stomach meds if you want some." They shuffled forward.

"Let's see how it goes now that I'm not in a moving vehicle."

Ellie nodded. "Okay. Just let me know."

Kate felt a bit guilty for lying, but she would not do anything to disrupt this trip for Ellie. It wouldn't be fair. She would tell Ellie when they got back on Sunday, or maybe even on the flight back home. It took all she had not to let it weigh her down. She was ultra-aware of the search journal tucked snugly in the fine leather bag on her shoulder. Her parents had suggested she take a backpack, but that, she thought, would make her look like a tourist. She wanted to blend in.

"I'm so excited that you've decided to become Italian." Ellie kept her eyes trained on the customer service desk where two agents were helping a line of passengers.

"That's not what I said." Kate scoffed. Ellie's eyes whipped toward her. "I want to explore what it means to be Italian. Who the Italian people are and what, if any, traits are a natural part of being Italian." A sick feeling hit her. What chance did she have of escaping the horrors of her heritage if her adoptive parents were also caught up in bad stuff? How could she escape both nature and nurture? Now that would be a real science project. Maybe she should suggest it to Colby.

"Fine," Ellie said, "but I don't think there's much difference. I bet you're going to discover that you love that part of you. But, listen. If you do discover you love your Italian side, you can't leave me and live there."

Kate laughed. "Don't be absurd. I couldn't stay if I wanted to."

"Good, 'cause I need you." She batted her long eyelashes at Kate.

"And I need you." Kate batted right back. "You're my best friend and I couldn't live without you."

"Ditto. But, if you found an Italian guy to marry, you'd have the cutest little Italian babies."

"I'm not even close to thinking about babies, Italian or not." She moved away from Ellie like she had rabies or something.

"Still, they'd be adorbs."

After boarding the plane, they settled quickly into their first class seats, courtesy of Ellie's parents' mileage upgrades. After dinner, they watched a movie before going to sleep. Neither of them wanted to face jet lag without at least six good hours of sleep on the plane. The flight attendant woke them as the plane descended into Heathrow Airport in London.

"It's a downright shame that we'll be in London for the next few hours and not get to go exploring." Kate moaned as they got ready to deplane.

"No kidding. It's an injustice, really." Ellie grabbed her bottled water and swallowed the last little bit.

They shuffled off the plane with their carryon luggage and hustled through Customs and then to their connecting flight, sneaking glances of the surrounding country through the windows as they went.

The plane ride from London to Italy wasn't that long and soon the dense, orangish-red roofs of Bologna stared up at Kate as she looked out over the city from the plane, the early morning light making everything seem bright. It was as if she was entering another world, far distant from her own and yet the beauty and foreignness of it dazzled her. The fourteen hour combined flight had been thirteen too many and Kate was excited to be on the ground again.

Kate stared at her phone. She needed to tell her parents they had arrived, but she couldn't think about either of her parents without those pictures teasing her. After quickly sending a text to her parents telling them she'd arrived, Kate inspected her white shorts to make sure they were still white and she hadn't spilled anything on them. She walked off the plane with her bag over her shoulder and rolling a suitcase behind her. She followed Ellie to Customs, and cringed a little seeing the welcome sign as they entered the cue: Bologna Guglielmo Marconi

Airport.

"I truly hope it's not some bad omen or something that we flew into an airport named after a Marconi. We better not run into any of them here."

"Hello. We're in Italy. If we don't run into Marconis and Bellinis here, it would be weird. Don't you think? They're like the perfect Italian names."

"It's still scary." Kate glanced at her phone, not really expecting her parents to text back since it was only one a.m. in the U.S., but wishing they would. She also hadn't heard from Johansen even though she'd left three more messages. She had a vague recollection of having nightmares while on the plane. She had hoped doubling up on her self-defense classes and working harder than ever would make them stop, but they hadn't. If only Johansen would call her back, maybe she could set her mind at ease.

"I think so too, but we only need to remember," Ellie said, looking at the sign too, "the Marconis you're hiding from are in New Jersey, not here."

"I guess, but still, it's creepy that the name of the very family that wanted to hurt me and did hurt my birth parents has their name on this airport." She couldn't help but worry about the apparent success of the Marconi family both in Italy and in the U.S. Perhaps the Marconis who had stayed behind in Italy were the good ones. "Wasn't there another airport we could have flown into?"

"No. This is the closest one to Bologna. It's right here. We've been over this."

Kate huffed. "It would be just my luck that the Jersey Marconis own this airport and have their big goons all over it." She swept her gaze around the area.

Ellie snorted. "Not likely." She lowered her voice. "Those bullies left Italy because they wanted to become important, right?"

"I guess." They breezed through Customs and went straight to the baggage claim, then hauled their luggage to the area marked for ground transportation. Kate whipped her head around after seeing a guy who looked eerily familiar, but on further examination she could see that he wasn't Galtem Marconi, just someone who looked like him. The man could have easily been his cousin. While the knowledge that it wasn't Galtem did calm her a bit, Kate hoped he hadn't told any of his relatives in Italy, should he have any, about her. A rush of uncertainty waved through her, and she questioned whether or not coming to Italy had been a smart move after all.

Humid, heavy air filled with exhaust fumes hit them the second they walked out of the airport, clogging Kate's throat and making it hard to breathe. The unpleasant smell of too many people in too small a place filled the air. She had thought it would smell like pastries and perfume for some reason.

Ellie walked straight up to a man holding a sign that said "Lambert". He immediately lowered it when he saw the two girls. The picture Ellie's mom had sent to the driving service must have made it easy for him to recognize them.

"Welcome to Bologna," the driver said in Italian and then repeated it in English. "Right this way." His rich accent brought back both good and bad memories from Kate's time in New Jersey. While Vinny and Duran didn't have heavy Italian accents, the man who'd questioned her in Jersey, her biological grandfather, had. The driver put their luggage in the trunk and helped them and their bags into the back seat of the luxury car. The smell of leather and some type of sweet cigar filled the air. Before he pulled away from the curb, he said, "I will now give you a quick tour of the city to help you get acclimated to Bologna. My partner or I will be at your disposal while you're here. I'm Devlin Marconi."

Kate sucked in a breath. The two girls gave each other a look, but didn't want to bring attention to the name and make him think anything was up, so Ellie said, "I love your accent."

"Thank you. It comes with the territory." He handed them some brochures and the girls started sifting through them.

"Look at this place," Ellie said. "We've got to go here." She waved a brochure of what looked like a medieval market in front of Kate.

"Don't look at those now," Devlin said. "You'll want to be looking out the windows as I show you the most beautiful place on earth. Look at them after I'm gone to help you remember what I show you." He drove the winding streets, telling them all about the ancient city. The differences between the U.S. and Italy were immediately apparent as they zipped along the extremely narrow streets of Bologna. The sprawling streets and wide open spaces of Texas and even New Jersey were a distant memory. They had obviously been an extravagance. The plethora of multi-colored stucco houses and people cruising the city on bikes captured Kate's attention. "Can you believe how many people are on bikes here?" Kate asked Ellie.

"I know. I swear there are more bikes than cars. It's kinda cool, don't you think?"

Kate did think it was cool. Had her birth parents not lived in the U.S., she could have been one of those bike-riding people. Eventually, they drove up a big hill and Devlin pointed out the outlines of the campus and the surrounding area as well as the famous Basilica. "You should come back up here with those brochures later today and locate all the many places you will want to visit. Make a list, you know?"

"We will for sure," Ellie said. "It's beautiful up here."

Kate's mind had wandered over thoughts of her heritage. Could she really belong to these people who had such a rich history? Perhaps, but as far as Colby's perverse choice connection, that was insane.

"Now, look at those," Devlin said, his accent along with the ancient surroundings making it impossible to forget they were in another world as he pulled their attention to the tall towers and porticos surrounding them. "You will find this is a city full of these beautiful porticos." He pointed out other architectural oddities, and every now and then Ellie would squeal with delight and clutch at Kate's arm as they passed something she recognized.

As they drove, Colby's words reached out, teasing and taunting Kate. *You'll be able to see where your people come from. I don't mean just your parents, but who you are as an Italian. Like we are from England and they're our people.* Maybe he had been right. Here, she could get to her roots and find out what made an Italian tick. And, she didn't need to only stick with the Italian collective. She could look into her ancestors, both adopted and birth. She hoped while she was here she could find out if Abrie's parents, Kate's adoptive grandparents, were truly terrible people too and if Abrie had had anything to do with it.

She really should uncover what it meant to be Italian. What it meant at a very basic level—the level of genes. She thought of the Germans and how inclined they were toward engineering. What were Italians inclined to be? Religious? Mafia? She shook her head trying to get the idea out. *You can find out who you are,* Colby had claimed. *And better understand why you do the things you do. It's all in your genes, you know?*

No. She had to believe she was in control of her choices. Her genes did not tell her what to choose, and she couldn't accept that her adoptive parents could claim that control either. She looked down at her hand and discovered was stroking the outside of her search journal still tucked away inside her bag. She jerked her hand away and clasped them together on her lap. Ellie gave her a concerned look, but Kate only smiled at her.

A few minutes later, Devlin interrupted her thoughts again, "We are now passing the Piazza Magiore. Peaceful, open, and lovely in every way. There will be tourists in there, but the greatest concentration of people will be locals." A few minutes later, he continued as they entered a different section of town. "This is the university district where you will be staying. Looks different when you're in the middle of it, doesn't it?" He drove several blocks and down a main street, pointing out this building or that, but jetlag was settling in and his words jumbled together. Kate needed to get out of the car.

"You mean this is the campus?" Ellie asked, incredulity coloring her words. "It seems more like a business district than a campus."

Kate perked up at this, noting the same things Ellie had. The

University of Bologna was nothing like the campuses back home with sprawling green lawns and obvious boundaries. The lack of green space made her feel compressed. People milled about everywhere. Streets were filled with cars and an equal number of if not more bikes, motorcycles, and mopeds. Ellie kept tapping Kate's leg and squealing every time they passed someone she deemed hot. Kate feigned interest, but in truth, she compared them all to Duran and found them lacking.

The once majestic columns and stone walls were covered with flapping advertisements and invitations. And graffiti littered every possible surface, words hastily painted, destroying the beautiful architecture and atmosphere.

"Is it safe here?" Kate asked, the marked walls and area making her feel unsure.

"Safe? Why, yes. Just beware of pickpockets and stay with your brother in the evenings. It is like any large city and one must be vigilant in keeping oneself safe. But, my brother and I are here for you this week, to take you where you need to go." Devlin pulled to an intersection and stopped and looked at them through his rearview mirror. He smiled. "Italy is a wonderful, beautiful place for you to visit."

It almost felt like Devlin should get a kickback from a Visit Italy campaign. Anything that had to be sold with a speech like that had problems for sure. Kate did not feel safe in the least and would not go gallivanting around on her own. Message received.

They approached an ancient looking light green stucco building with about fifteen stairs leading up to a maroon door and pulled into a free spot along the street. "We have luck today. The Gods are smiling at us."

Kate assumed Devlin was talking about the free parking space so near Colby's apartment, because it seemed all spots everywhere were filled with cars. His mention of God also calmed her.

As soon as the two girls climbed out of the car, Colby and six other guys came tumbling out of the apartment to greet them. "It's about time. Devlin must've forced you on his 'quick' tour of Bologna."

"Hey, now. Don't be cheeky. I always get my charges where they need to go." It was funny to hear him speak English with both a British English accent and an Italian one mixed together.

As Devlin unloaded their luggage, he added, "If there's anything you ladies need, let me know." And he meant it, Kate could tell. She already liked this Italian man. Despite his name, she hoped there were others just like him. She'd made up her mind. The Marconis in Italy were good.

Colby hugged Ellie first and then Kate. He acted like he hadn't seen either of them in months or even years and it'd been less than a week. They laughed as the other boys from all over the world introduced themselves. For ease, Kate called each one by their country of origin. Canada, England, Germany, Finland, America, and the Netherlands. They rushed the girls indoors and led them to a room with one small twin bed and a pallet on the floor. The room was the size of Kate's closet back home.

"You'll be nice and cozy in there, wontcha?" Colby said, grinning. "I'll be on the couch."

"You're kidding, right?" Kate sat on the bed, thinking about unpacking and realizing there was nowhere to unpack. Ellie must've realized the same thing, because they shared a look and then busted out laughing.

Colby called out from the living room, "We've got to get back to class. Eat whatever you can find. There's a map of the campus on the table for you to explore. I suggest a hike up to the basilica. It's awesome. There's an envelope from Mom with some euros in it for you guys to use while here. Some places don't like to take cards." The door slammed behind the guys and the girls emerged from their tiny room.

The kitchen was a holly hobby type with a stove and oven about a third the size of one in the States although it did boast two burners, one small and one large. The fridge was small too, and almost empty. The boys probably ate out for almost every meal. There were some old pastries, oatmeal, and yogurt, none of which sounded appetizing at all.

61

Cindy M. Hogan

Ellie put the money in her wallet while Kate picked up the map, which was really a brochure for the university and looked it over. The university was amazing. More like several city blocks. Several ancient city blocks.

"I'd really like to hike up the hill like Colby suggested, but I'm starving and there's nothing here to eat." Kate went to their room and grabbed their bags.

"Let's go find a café and get some real Italian food." Ellie clapped her hands. "We can sit and watch people and talk with locals."

"Yeah," Kate said, grabbing Ellie's hands. "Let's go see what it means to be Italian. Wahoo. So excited." She forced her glee over lingering worry from the pictures. She had to make up for the awful trip to Jersey.

Kate grinned and handed Ellie her bag, which she slung over her shoulder. Kate did the same with hers. "This is going to be a lot of fun. Remember what we talked about. You can't keep pining over Duran."

"I know." Kate said it, but she didn't really agree with the words.

"Besides," Ellie said as she walked to the door. "This is a university. That means guys our age. Hot Italian guys."

"You mean guys three to five years older than we are."

Ellie waved her hand, dismissing Kate's comment.

They stopped at the third café they saw and sat and ate pasta and sauce with a crusty roll. They weren't exactly sure what the sauce was, but it was delicious. They also flirted with several boys who came by, but they all happened to be tourists. "This doesn't seem like an authentic Italian experience. Where can we go that is tourist free?"

"Considering that tourism is one of the main industries in Italy, I'm not sure there's anywhere we can go. It's probably worse right here because of the university. At least the food is authentic. Let's get out of here."

They walked aimlessly for a bit.

"I can't believe how much graffiti there is here and it's not pretty graffiti either." Ellie locked arms with Kate and they headed down the busy street.

"I know. Maybe that's what you get when you're in a college town of like sixty thousand students." Kate avoided some trash on the sidewalk.

"If they wanted to make a statement, you'd think they'd make it beautiful so people would pay attention and want to look at it." She made a sound like a cat crying. "Oh, Kate, I so want to paint right now."

"This is good for you. You can learn some moderation in your addiction." Kate had her phone out, trying to figure out where exactly they were. "We're at the border of the university. It's crazy that the university just looks like a bunch of city blocks."

"It's beautiful. I can't wait to get inside some of these buildings." Ellie looked wistful. "What's next on the To Do list?"

Kate also couldn't wait to paint pictures of the buildings. "Well, we ate all that yummy food, why don't we do the San Luca hike back up to the Basilica."

"Alright."

They took a short taxi ride to the San Luca Portico trailhead and hiked up, leaving the mass of buildings to the green of the hills.

"Well look who we have here," a good looking Italian guy said when they'd only gone a meter or so. "A couple of hot American girls." He and the other three guys with him seemed to leer at them, so Ellie grabbed hold of Kate and hurried past only to hear several whistles call after them.

"I like attention as much as the next girl, but that was pretty creepy."

Before Kate could respond, a tall, tan skinned man, who had to be in his forties whistled at them and said, "Bella."

"Back off, creeper," Ellie said.

"I thought you liked older guys," Kate said, laughing.

"Why are you laughing? We are not pieces of meat." She glared at Kate, who continued to grin.

"Sorry, Ellie. It's an Italian thing."

"Oh, now you're claiming to be Italian."

"No," she chuckled. "Italian men whistle to show their appreciation for good-looking women. I read about it online. It's not considered an insult like it is back home."

"Serious?"

"Yes. So you can stop being offended."

A couple more whistles filtered over to them. "I don't know. This may take some getting used to."

"Yeah. It goes against our sensibilities."

"Definitely, but I'm going to have to get over it. Check out those beautiful guys ahead."

Kate couldn't miss them. It seemed most of the guys they had seen had been attractive in one way or another. Before the guys could whistle, Ellie introduced herself. She was back in the saddle.

"Ellie," one tall blond said in an unfamiliar accent. "You are from America, no?"

Kate frowned, but Ellie brightened. "Yep. On vacation. You from here?"

"We are all here for school." He jerked his head to his four companions. "These are my flatmates."

"Oh." The guys listed the cities they were from. Ellie asked them a couple more questions and when the blond wouldn't stop touching her, she grabbed hold of Kate and pulled her up the hill telling them they were on a schedule.

"I think you may have met your match, Ellie Lambert," Kate said. "Italian boys are forward for sure." The majority of people they met the rest of the way up the three-kilometer trail to the Sanctuary of the Madonna di San Luca were either tourists or students. It became a little game for them to guess which were which. A whistle usually made the determination for them. Most of the people they met were very friendly and forthright. The cement trail boasted an arcade, a covered walkway enclosed by a line of arches on one or both sides of the walkway. It was one of the longest in the world with 666 arches. The brochure Devlin had given them told them it had been built to protect the icon of the virgin as they brought it up to the basilica.

The basilica was surrounded by a lush forest and Kate sucked in a breath at the beauty of it all. They walked around the peaceful, ornate building, checking out its many nooks and crannies. "You ready to walk back down?" Kate asked Ellie once they made it back outside.

"Not really. I mean, we'll run into the same kinds of people. College students and tourists."

"I thought you were keen on all the hot college students."

"I am." She grinned. "But I'd really like to peek into more of an established Italian person's life. I mean seriously, think about an Italian learning about our culture from a teenager."

Kate chuckled. That sounded pretty weird, but she knew what Ellie was trying to say.

"We could go to Piazza Magiore that we drove by and that Devlin suggested had more locals than tourists." She whipped out a brochure about it. "It says here that it is a market square from the 15th century."

"Good idea." Kate had wanted to go there after Devlin's description of it too.

"First, let's stop by the medieval section of town and see what there is to buy and see. It's supposed to be pretty cool. It's farther away, but we can cut back through the Piazza on our way back to the apartment."

"Medieval, huh? I'm game. I'll be taking lots of pictures. I'd like to paint a medieval scene, I think."

"There's supposed to be great shopping and lots of good stuff to eat. Chocolate and stuff."

"Yum."

8

While at first glance the market seemed authentic, it quickly became apparent that it was a tourist trap. There were fresh noodles of all sorts, but it was full of tourists and jam-packed with tons of students looking for a cheap meal. "This is nothing like how I'd imagined," Ellie said. "And the smell. I'm not sure I can take much more." The smell of raw fish and meat mixed with the scents of those that had been smoked was not a pleasant one.

"Yeah. I'm not really interested in sausages. We're going to hit students everywhere we go, there are so many here, but I'm hoping there will be a minimal number at the piazza." Kate made a mental note to return and pick up some fresh pastas to take home with her at the end of their trip.

"At least the chocolate was good," Ellie said, putting another truffle into her mouth.

They used a maps app to lead the way to the piazza and struck out on foot. The narrow roads led the way to the large, cobbled open area with little shops and eateries encircling it. They paused just inside the open area, both taking a deep breath and looking at each other and smiling before continuing. The piazza was quiet and beautiful. Doves and other birds swooped and landed, hoping to grab a morsel of dropped food. Waiters in crisp white and black uniforms served the many sections of open air seating, bringing and taking away food and drink to patrons. A few benches were scattered about, all already claimed. Those not seated at a café or restaurant milled about, browsing through wares that spilled out of shops onto the sidewalks, or window shopped in no apparent hurry. Others walked casually in small groups, chatting and laughing. Many of the benches were occupied by old men and women who threw birdseed for the many birds. Couples occupied the others. Love was in the air and it made Kate's heart rush every now and then as she thought of Duran.

An old couple walked by holding hands. "You see," Kate mused, "if this is what it means to be Italian, I have no problem with it." Kate grinned until it hurt her cheeks.

"Do you feel like a part of you has become whole? Kinda like finding your dad?" Ellie leaned into Kate with her shoulder.

"I don't know if it's the same, but I do feel a sort of pull toward these people, whether it's because Colby told me I should, or if I really do." A stray thought about her mom's dad whipped through her mind and she shoved it back into a corner. She wasn't sure how long she could keep the secret from Ellie.

"Let's choose the romantic notion and go with it. You feel the pull." Ellie winked at Kate. "Wouldn't it be fun if there was an injection that could make you feel what they feel inside? Feel truly Italian for one day? See if you liked how it felt." She grinned and then said, "Check that out." She motioned with her head to a gelato stand where a line of guys stood ordering and eating gelato. "I think I feel the need for some gelato." She elbowed Kate.

"Yum," Kate said, thinking of the gelato and not the guys. Ever since Jersey and Jace, Kate had been more cautious when it came to guys and flings, not that she had ever really experienced a fling besides the one with Jace. She recognized that despite what a person portrayed on the outside, it was hard to tell what was going on inside. She still hadn't completely forgiven herself for how she'd treated Jace that last day even

Cindy M. Hogan

though deep down she knew she wasn't to blame for his actions. He'd had a lot going on in his life and hadn't been truly happy for a very long time. Nonetheless, she would be careful and make sure she was clear about her expectations, how she felt, and what the guy should expect from her from now on.

Ellie started over after she grabbed Kate's hand and pulled her along. True to form, Ellie didn't go to the back of the line, she walked right up to the guys and said, "*Ciao!*"

Several of the guys said, "*Ciao!*" right back and looked her up and down and then moved on to Kate. Her face immediately heated up and she looked at her shoes.

Ellie tilted her head and said, "Any good flavors today?"

One of the guys moved forward and winked. "Would you like to try mine?" His Italian accent was thick, his voice deep.

"Depends on what it is. I was thinking something with chocolate today."

"Nutella," the tallest of the group said, stepping forward at the same time a dark blond with brown eyes moved toward them. "Stracciatella is perfecto for you."

Truly, Ellie could make any guy swoon with her beach tan body and blond hair. She looked at all the different choices and then at the guys who offered them and said, looking at the guy, not the gelato, "Stracciatella it is." The guy smiled and held it out for her to taste. "Could you order my friend and me one? There's no way I could tell her the name."

He smiled. "Yes." And they followed him to the line. While standing there, the first guy who'd spoken moved toward Kate. "You are Americans?"

"Is it that obvious?" Kate said, wishing her face would cool off already. It seemed everyone they had run into today had known they were Americans.

"Well, you speak American English, not British English."

"Oh, yeah," Kate said. "I thought maybe something about how we

68

dress or act screamed American."

"Maybe a little, but that's okay. You actually look Italian, though. I'm Martino."

"Maybe because I am. I'm Kate." She was shocked that the words had so easily tumbled out.

His head jerked back. "But you don't speak Italian?"

"I was adopted." She searched his eyes to see his reaction. They moved slowly closer to the gelato stand and where Ellie and her guy, whose name Kate overheard was Constantin, were talking and laughing away. The rest of the other guys continued to eat their treats standing off to the side.

"Ah. So you are here on holiday?" She didn't catch any hesitance from him.

She nodded. "Yeah. I'd really like to get a feel for how Italians are. To see if I'm like them."

"You think all Italians are the same?" Martino grinned like he was about to eat a whole cheesecake.

Kate didn't want to go into the whole gene thing. "No, but you knew we were American even before we spoke, I bet."

"Yes. I did."

"But why?" They shuffled forward as the line moved. "That's the question, right? What is it that tips people off that I'm American and you're Italian?"

"I could show you Italy." Martino's smile was kind and inviting. "How long are you here?"

"Only a few days, unfortunately. You think I can get a good taste of what it means to be Italian in only a few days?"

"I think you can get a taste." He winked. "I'd love to help you with that." Kate's whole body reacted with lovely tingles in response to his words, but her mind was yelling at her to be careful. What kind of a guy would want to spend serious time with a girl when he knew it would only be for a few days? Ellie ordered and paid. Kate thought about her promise to Ellie that she would open up while in Italy and not let her memories of Duran keep her from making other connections. Her heart thumped with a sense of betrayal and loss, but she said, "I'd like that," ignoring the feelings. Nothing serious would happen in two days anyway.

It was their turn to order and Martino bent over and whispered the words she'd need to say, his fingers resting on her forearms. He smelled musky and somehow fruity at the same time. Kate sucked in a breath and repeated what he'd said.

The server raised her eyebrows and looked at Martino. He bent back down and repeated the phrase for ordering again, only he stopped in the middle. Kate repeated what he'd said and then he whispered the rest and she repeated that. Their server smiled and scooped three big scoops of gelato onto a cone for her.

"Whoa! That's too much."

"Lesson number one: Being Italian means doing it big and doing it right." His thick, enticing accent helped imprint his words on her soul.

Kate smiled and started in on the treat as they left the stand to meet up with the rest of the group. Martino kept a strong hand on her elbow, leading her.

Everyone made comments about the size of her cone and laughed, their hands flying all over the place as they spoke. Martino leaned down and whispered, "Lesson number two: We like to be seen and heard."

Kate chuckled. "So do Americans." She glanced at her feet. He moved in front of her and looked her in the eyes, separating her from the others but only by a few feet. "Number three: As an Italian, you should never be ashamed of who you are or what you are doing. Being Italian means being proud to be Italian. You belong to a people influenced by some of the most *interessante* cultures throughout history."

As he spoke, she could feel how deeply he believed what he said. The Italian accent slid over her skin like a sweet caress, and she wanted desperately to feel the same way. His deep brown eyes seemed to see into her soul. So far she liked what it meant to be Italian.

She stood straighter and smiled. "Wow. Three lessons in such a short time. How many lessons are there exactly?" She was dying for more. Through him, she believed she truly could discover her Italian-ness.

"That depends on you." He quirked up one corner of his mouth. Fire raced to her heart. She'd never met anyone as charming. At least not that would talk to her and act interested in her.

"We hope you two enjoy Italy," one of the guys in the group said. "But we must go to class." He gave a meaningful look to Martino and Constantin. Ellie pouted.

"How about dinner tonight?" Martino asked, his smooth voice begging her to say yes.

"Actually," Kate said, leaning around him to look at Ellie. "We already have plans. Tomorrow?"

"Tomorrow is dinner with family." He narrowed his eyes like he was thinking. "Yes. Lesson number four: Family is everything, but of course you should help others whenever you can. Would you like to have the most *incredibile* meal of your life tomorrow?"

"How could I say no to that?" Her insides quaked and she had to be careful not to squeeze the cone in her hand too hard.

"Excellent. Lesson number five: Eating Italian food is a *sensuale* experience, meant to be savored. And if you didn't catch it, lesson number six is: Italians are very hospitable. Where should I pick you up?"

"Ellie will need to come with me if that's okay."

"Sure." He turned to Constantin. "Constantin, can you be there?"

He nodded and leaned down to kiss Ellie on both her cheeks, his lips brushing hers as he moved from one to the other. A bit of fear sneaked into Kate's heart.

"In that case, how about I call you at five and let you know where to pick us up?"

Martino grabbed her into a hug and whispered, "Can I have your number too?"

She nodded and put her number into his phone, working hard not to let her fingers shake as she did. Was he going to try to kiss her like Constantin had with Ellie? She wasn't sure she was ready for that. He took back his phone and dialed her number. She answered and added his name into her phone. "I'll call. Be ready to have a meal prepared from scratch with *amore* and care." He smiled and then squeezed her hands. She stiffened, not sure what was coming next. When nothing did, she let out a long, shallow breath as he walked away. She thought of all the videos she'd seen with Italians in them. This dinner was sure to be interesting. Martino had been pretty touchy and it seemed grandmas and aunts liked to kiss everyone and grab cheeks and stuff. Maybe she could get out of it somehow.

Martino, Constantin, and the rest of them sauntered away, and Ellie fanned herself. "They were so hot, Kate. We have dates with gorgeous Italian guys."

Kate frowned. "Yes we do. Yes we do. What do you think they will say when they discover we are still in high school?"

"They aren't going to. We are nineteen while here in Italy."

"We are, are we?"

They stared after the guys until they were out of sight. She didn't dare tell Ellie at that moment about how scared she was for the date. Instead, she shared the six lessons Martino taught her about Italians because she knew Ellie would love it. They swooned a bit as she spoke.

"And the other lessons he's going to pass on?" She gave Kate a knowing look.

"Stop it. Nothing will happen between us. There isn't enough time. We have to leave in a few days." Kate tried to convince herself that everything would be okay. If she backed out of dinner now, Ellie would be so sad. Kate had already ruined Ellie's last vacation. Kate wasn't about to ruin another. She would play along, but be careful what signals she gave Martino. She would keep him in the friend zone.

An older couple walked past, hand in hand. A young couple laughed and talked loudly as they meandered fifteen feet away. It seemed at that moment everyone in the piazza were couples. A grin spread across her face. "And number seven," Ellie said, reading her mind. "Italians are not only passionate about food, they are also passionate about love."

Kate forced a giggle. "I guess you'll see just how much tomorrow, won't you?"

"I think it'll be you finding that out before me," Ellie said. Kate stiffened and she felt a bit of pain in her chest. She looked at the mound of gelato still in her cone and headed for a trashcan where she tossed it. There was no way she could have eaten it all. They made their way to an open bench and sat to watch and absorb the Italian spirit.

As Kate sat watching the people pass by, laughing and talking animatedly, subconsciously she fingered the locket around her neck, trying to imagine her birth mother and father there. Trying to imagine being there as a baby, held by her birth mother just like in the picture in the locket. All thoughts of Martino fled.

Ellie grabbed her arm. "Kate. Hello! Earth to Kate."

Kate blinked several times and tried to clear her head. "Yeah."

"What were you thinking about? I've been trying to get your attention forever. You totally missed it." Ellie's eyes fell to the locket in Kate's fingers. "Wait a minute. The locket."

9

Kate's hand fell from the locket. "What?"

"Your locket. It's from Italy."

"So?"

"Maybe we can find out where your birth parents bought it."

"And what would that do for me?"

"You could ask the person who made it questions about your mother." Ellie's eyes grew to the size of walnuts as she spoke.

"Ellie, what are the chances that we'll find the jeweler who made this particular locket?" Kate gave her friend a seriously-there's-no-chance look.

"I think pretty high because this is a special piece." That surprised Kate. "It was never mass produced." Ellie touched the locket. "It's an expensive piece of jewelry. I'm betting this little beauty is a signature piece people will recognize." She grabbed Kate's hands. "What do you have to lose? Seriously. I can see four or five jewelry stores right here that we can check. If nothing comes of it, no big deal, right?"

Fire burned in Kate's belly. She sighed. "But, I already decided to stop looking for my birth mother. It's too painful."

"Why did you bring the notebook then?"

"Don't rub it in." She hadn't realized Ellie knew about the journal, but she should have known she couldn't keep that from Ellie.

"It's only painful when you run into a dead end. This opens doors, it doesn't close them." Ellie put her hand on Kate's.

Kate didn't know what to say. She knew Ellie was putting a positive spin on things. It very well could end up making her hopeful only to make her crash in the end. She didn't want to risk it. Understanding her Italian heritage was one thing, but finding her birth mother was another.

"I don't know, Ellie. Remember what happened last time? What if something like that happens again?"

"This is Carmela. Hello. The FBI agent."

"But, she's not. If she was, Special Agent Johansen would have found her."

"Come on. You've been dying to find your birth mother for so long. This is your one last opportunity. Look at it like that. Five jewelry stores. We're throwing up a prayer here. Besides, I could do with some more jewelry."

"Fine. But, only the five stores." Kate figured she wouldn't have time to really hope if there were only five stores to ask.

"Yes!" Ellie said, squealing and bouncing on the bench. "You won't be sorry. Come on. Let's go." Ellie still loved a mystery. Kate figured that would never change.

Kate's heart beat hard and wild in her chest and she felt a bit weak, but with Ellie leading the charge, she grabbed hold of her courage she needed to keep walking.

The first three stores gave them nothing. Despite that, the shopkeepers were kind, suave, and knew on sight they were Americans, just like the guys they'd eaten gelato with had.

"Does it bother you that everyone somehow knows we're Americans?" Kate asked Ellie.

"No. I love that. It sets me apart and makes people notice me."

"But we're here to observe and hopefully absorb the Italian culture."

"You have a point there."

"How about we go clothes shopping and ask for help to become less obtrusive." Kate wasn't sure any change in clothes would hide the fact that Ellie was an American, but she was willing to try.

"After the jewelry stores, you're not getting out of your promise. You said five and we are going to five jewelry stores."

Kate stopped in her tracks. "I'm willing to go to the final two." Her stomach clenched at the thought. "Nothing's going to come of it, but I'm serious about the new clothes. I really want to fit in and pretend to be Italian."

"You are Italian, but I like how you think. After the jewelry stores, it's clothes shopping time."

The next two jewelry stores stood right next to each other. The girls stared at the two shops. "Let's hit the ancient looking place first."

"Yeah. I think it's our last chance. The other place looks like it only carries cheap tourist goods."

Kate nodded. "I'm so excited about getting some real Italian clothes." She was thrilled about it, but would also need something to keep her mind off Carmela and the fact that she hadn't found any information about her. Hope had seeped into her soul as they'd questioned the shop owners even though she hadn't wanted it to.

"Me, too. Now's a good time for you say a word up to that god of yours."

Kate grimaced, but couldn't help herself. She thought a quick prayer and heat spread through her gut. After a deep breath, she followed Ellie into the shop.

A tall, thin guy with red hair and pasty white skin full of large freckles greeted them right off. "*Ciao* and welcome." He spoke Italian, but he had red hair. He couldn't truly be Italian. Maybe this would be a dead end after all.

"*Ciao*," Ellie parroted. "Guess we stand out as Americans."

"*Bellisimo.* I'm Gallo and I'm glad to assist you. Come look at these—"

"Sorry. We have a question first."

He nodded.

"Do you have any idea where this came from?" Ellie pointed at the locket around Kate's neck.

"Could I maybe get a closer look?" He was the first one to ask to see it. Maybe this would prove promising.

Kate nodded as she unclasped the locket and handed it to him. "Are you Italian?" Kate couldn't help herself.

"What makes you think I'm not?" His eyes gleamed with mischief.

"Maybe the red hair."

Gallo chuckled. "I was adopted, but yes, I'm Italian, through and through."

"You were adopted?" Kate looked at him in surprise.

"What else would explain this?" he said, pointing to his red, curly hair.

"Sorry. I'm adopted too, but my parents were Italian." She looked at Ellie who was grinning.

"That's nuts, right? That you were adopted into an American family and I was adopted into an Italian one. If I weren't significantly older and a different gender, then I'd have to scream foul play. But, my, you do look Italian."

"I bet you're asked every day."

"I am. Almost."

"Where are your birth parents from?"

"No clue and I don't want to know." Surety sat in his voice and eyes.

"Really? Why not?"

"It's not like knowing where my parents are from would change anything. I am who I am. I am Italian."

"What if you found out your birth parents are English?"

"It wouldn't change anything."

"Do you think it might help you understand who you are?" Kate couldn't still her curiosity. He really didn't care who his birth parents were.

"Not at all. I have control over who I choose to be and knowing the origin of my parents wouldn't change that."

Ellie cleared her throat. "All very interesting." Kate figured she didn't want this salesperson to deter her from the importance of finding Carmela. "But, we were hoping to get some information about that piece of jewelry in your hand." He stared at it as if he'd just now noticed what he was holding.

"Ah, yes. This is before my time. Let me see." He looked it over, making a few little noises of appreciation and then saying, "This is a fine piece."

Kate nodded. "But it's not from here?" Relief and sadness washed through her simultaneously.

"No, but I think I might know someone who might know where it is from." Kate kept waiting for his accent to sound different than the ones she'd already heard, but it sounded the same. He sure seemed Italian.

"Really?"

"There's no guarantee, but maybe." He handed the locket back to Kate.

"Okay." Kate pressed her lips together in appreciation. "That's all we can hope for." Gallo left them, going into a back room.

The two girls browsed the jewelry cases until he returned, an older gentleman in tow.

The older gentleman was stooped and full-on gray, but had a twinkle in his eye when he saw the two girls.

"Ladies, this is Manfredo."

Manfredo spoke, but in Italian. Gallo interpreted for him.

"So, you have a lovely locket, do you?"

"*Si.*" Kate held it out to him. They took the remaining two steps forward and he took the locket from her. "*Uh. Si. Bueno. Uh, huh. Mmm.*" From there Manfredo shuffled behind the cases of jewelry and brought out a leather tool roll and untied it, revealing small tools of all sorts. He spoke again and Gallo continued to translate. "Do you mind?" The old man held out a metal looking pick.

"What is he going to do?" Kate moved toward the locket in one big jerk, her voice wavering and her mouth drying out.

"Open it up."

Kate looked at Ellie, who nodded. "Maybe there's a signature inside or something."

"Go ahead." Kate nodded once. Her skin tingled as sweat began to form on her brow.

Manfredo used the tool to carefully pry open the portion of the locket behind the picture. Kate hadn't even realized it could be opened. The old man placed a small magnifying glass in front of one eye and examined the opened locket. "*Sì. Bueno.*" He smiled and continued to look while speaking in rapid Italian for a few seconds before setting both the locket and the magnifier down on the counter. He spoke quickly and gesticulated and smiled and laughed. Gallo took on the old man's same mannerisms as he told them what was being said, translating for both the girls and the old man the rest of the time.

"It was made by a man he apprenticed with. A lovely man. He would know his work anywhere, but he had to confirm it. The man is gone. Dead."

Kate's heart sank despite having told herself not to hope. It had been impossible after all.

Ellie asked the first question. "Did he ever ship them to America?"

"No, they were only sold in Italy." Ellie swung her hip into Kate in triumph.

"Few were ever made. The shop is in Venice. It's still there. Run by the son." The old man began cleaning the locket with fine tipped tools and a couple of different cloths.

"Um," Kate said, not knowing if she should be worried.

"It's okay," Gallo said. "He's cleaning it for you. He will polish it and it will be like new. He'd like to honor his old master by doing this."

Kate wasn't sure she wanted the locket clean and shiny. She really liked how it had a vintage look about it, but the old man looked so delighted and seemed to be taking such care with the item, that she let him.

Gallo spoke up. "Venice is only a few hours by train. A day trip from here if you want to go. You could talk to the son. I'm sure he's worked there all his life. "

Kate looked at Ellie who shrugged. "I've always wanted to go to Venice. Now we have a good excuse. We could get away from the college scene. The graffiti, the angst. Let's go to Venice. The city of love and canals. We can ride in a gondola and all of that."

Kate frowned. The locket. It wasn't a dead end yet. "Excuse us for just a moment." Kate took Ellie's arm and led her a few steps from Gallo and whispered. "I don't know, Ellie. The guy who made the locket is dead. His son owns the shop now. He won't remember my parents even if he ever met them."

"Don't be a pessimist, Kate. This isn't like you. What are you so afraid of?"

"Hello! Remember what happened when we followed the trail to my birth father? I can't put you into any more danger."

"We already addressed this. Just because Vinny is a bad guy doesn't mean Carmela is. I choose to think she's a good person and who knows, maybe she's the one who saved you when you were a baby."

"But if she was so good, why wouldn't Vinny have told me about her?"

"I can't answer that and since he wasn't willing to share, you need to find the answers yourself."

The spark that had lit inside Kate two years ago flickered back to life and an excited ache formed in her chest. She did want to find Carmela. Desperately. But, Carmela could be a bad person like her father. She could be dead. Kate wasn't sure she could handle either of those findings. She looked at Ellie's hopeful eyes and nodded. "Okay. We'll go. But I'm scared, and I don't want to put you in danger."

"Let's talk about this later." Ellie looked over at the counter where Manfredo was now putting the locket back together. He was humming to himself as he did. "He's almost done. Let's get the address or name or whatever we need to find the shop."

Kate nodded and asked for the information from Gallo. Manfredo moved from behind the counter and carefully, lovingly even, he put the locket around her neck and clasped it. He then took her by the upper arms and leaned in to kiss each of her cheeks, telling her something in Italian. She smiled. This man truly had loved his old master. "Thank you," was all Kate could say. The man's smiling eyes caused hers to burn and she had to look away to stop the tears from coming. She had a solid lead and despite her agreement with Ellie, she couldn't shake the fear she felt. She couldn't shake the thought that following this locket could lead her onto a dangerous path. A path that she might regret ever getting on. Gallo returned with a piece of paper on which he'd written the information about the other jeweler and handed it to Kate. Ellie was looking at some things in one of the jewelry cases. "Thank you."

"My pleasure." He smiled and she had this sudden urge to hug both Gallo and Manfredo, but she held back.

"Do you think I could look at these right here?" Ellie said from across the room.

"Certainly," Gallo said, giving Kate one last kind look.

While Ellie bought a ring and a necklace, Kate got restless, wanting nothing more than to get out of there. She looked at the locket that now shone with a brilliance she hadn't dreamed it could possess. It seemed to mirror the brightness of the excitement she felt at coming one step closer to finding her birth mother. A pressing feeling of claustrophobia had set in though and she had to keep glancing outside to keep herself from bursting out into the sunshine. She needed to find Carmela. To help the time pass, she thought she'd text her mom and dad, but found a text from Johansen instead.

Johansen: Sorry, Kate. I've been somewhere without access to my phone. I should have given you my partner's number. I just wasn't expecting to hear from you. I have nothing new to tell you. I'm guessing you're already in Italy. I would have discouraged you from going there all things considered, but I can see how you would love it there. Be careful.

Try not to stand out."

She texted him back.

Kate: What do you mean "all things considered?" What things?

Then she texted her mom and included her dad into the conversation

Mom: So glad you arrived safely. What have you been up to today?

Kate wasn't about to share the news about the locket and Carmela. She hadn't digested everything for herself yet. And, she wasn't sure they were going to end up in Venice. Not really.

Kate: We ate some amazing pasta at a quaint café. Hiked up through a bunch of arches to get to a cool church, went to a medieval market (too touristy), and right now we're at a piazza and Ellie's shopping for jewelry.

Mom: Sounds lovely.

Kate: It is beautiful here. Could do without the graffiti, but other than that, it's spectacular.

Mom: Send pictures please.

Kate: Will do. Ellie's done. Gotta go.

Mom: We love you. Stay safe.

Gallo took the same care with the jewelry Ellie picked out, carefully examining and cleaning it before putting it on her. He obviously loved his trade. He had been taught by a master and was his own master now.

Ellie took pictures of both men. She knew Kate would want to put pictures of the shop into her search journal as soon as possible.

They spent the next couple of hours shopping for Italian clothes and learning their next couple of lessons about being Italian.

Number nine: Italians love to give constructive criticism. And if you ask advice about buying clothes to fit in as an Italian, you should be prepared to receive advice about everything else.

And as for the clothes, that lead to number ten: Italians dress gaudy and glamorously, but the fabrics and the quality are amazing.

They sat on a bench while Kate entered all the information she'd learned from Gallo and Manfredo, making sure to spell the name of the shop correctly in her journal. She tried not to think about Venice. Ellie drew the outside of the shop on the opposite page and then took a picture. Kate and Ellie smiled as they made their way back to the apartment with bags of new clothes and costume jewelry and a sense that they would finally fit in.

10

The guys returned to the apartment shortly after the girls. "Go change. We're heading to dinner."

"Do Italians dress up for dinner?" Ellie asked.

Colby nodded. "And after we show you around campus, we'll be heading to a party." He waggled his eyebrows.

"We have some things to tell you, Colby," Kate said. She really wished she could talk to him about the pictures of the dead people, but that would have to wait.

"We can talk at dinner, okay? I need to change."

"Okay." The girls were excited to wear one of the outfits they'd bought on the piazza. After changing and getting freshened up, they walked out of the tiny room and the guys whistled. The girls played it up, spinning for them. The guys had been in Italy less than a week and had already caught onto that cultural norm.

"Let's go!" Spain said.

"We're going to a little café down the road. We eat there a lot. Great food." Colby put his arm around Kate. "You're going to love it."

"Yeah. You must only eat out. I mean, you have no food in this place." Ellie folded her arms across her chest.

"Sorry about that, but we've really had no time to do any grocery shopping. Everything is closed when we get out of class."

As promised, the café was not far and it was packed, but it didn't matter. The guys walked right up to a table that looked full and sat down. Everyone just squished up together and made room. Unlike in the States there wasn't one table per group of customers; if there was an open spot, anyone could sit there and apparently, if there wasn't a spot, they'd make one.

"Pretty cool, huh?" Colby said. "No more waiting. Sit by me."

Italians' definition of space was very different from Americans'. And it was loud. While Kate couldn't understand much of what was being said, the atmosphere was happy and full of life.

"What do you want?" Colby asked.

"What is there?" Ellie and Kate looked at a menu, but it was all in Italian.

"Every pasta and sauce you could think of. The servers can understand you if you speak in English."

"We had pasta for lunch."

"You'll eat pasta for every meal here," England said and they all laughed.

"I thought Italy was known for its pizza."

"It is, just not at this café. We can have pizza another night."

After ordering various pastas and sauces including a Ragu, a specialty of the area, everyone talked with varying degrees of English proficiency as they tried to understand each other. The food was made fresh to order and came slowly. Very slowly. Kate looked around the room, soaking up the atmosphere and trying to embrace this new idea of personal space. It made her nervous at first, but after twenty minutes or so, she was able to relax and enjoy herself. When the food came, it was delicious. The crusty bread rounded off the experience. She couldn't help wondering why Americans didn't eat crusty bread regularly like they did here. Kate focused on savoring every bite and not hurrying.

"What did you want to tell me?" Colby asked. The room still boomed with conversation.

He was so close and Kate liked how he seemed to have taken her under his wing. "It's so loud in here. It can wait."

An hour and a half after arriving, they got up to leave. Kate turned and then whipped her head toward the back of the restaurant where the servers came and went from the kitchen. She thought she saw one of the girls from the Marconi club in Jersey, but when she turned back all she could see was the back of the girl as the door shut behind her. No. It wasn't. It couldn't have been. Cold dread pumped through Kate's veins even though she thought her mind was playing tricks on her.

Ellie grabbed her arm and Kate stopped staring at the closed door. "What's up? You look like you saw a ghost."

"I thought I did for a second there. This girl from..." She let her words trail off as her eyes fell on Ellie. "It was nothing. She was nobody." Kate didn't want to tell Ellie what she thought she'd seen because after she'd gotten back from New Jersey, she had thought she had seen lots of different Marconis and Bellinis around every corner, fear of them finding her and taking control.

"Everyone is already outside. Come on."

Kate nodded. Just great, now she was hallucinating. What next? But, Colby wasn't outside, he was standing next to the door, holding it open for them. "You okay?"

"Yeah. It was stupid."

The guys were obviously all pumped, ready to go to the party, talking loudly, laughing, and posturing. As soon as the three of them joined the others, they started down the sidewalk.

"It's still a little early to show up at the party. We'll give you a tour of the campus as we go. The party is clear on the opposite end. Keep your hand on your purse and don't get too close to anyone or you will lose your stuff for sure." Colby gave them a warning look. With the mass of students attending the university, it seemed a very daunting task to maintain law and order.

Both Kate and Ellie grabbed hold of their bags, pressing them close to their bodies. Colby focused on the older university buildings centered along Via Zamboni, along with lots of other pubs, cafés and pizzerias. The whole area was plastered with posters and advertisements searching for or offering rooms, selling or buying something, or promoting any kind of event or party. It was quite dirty and there were a lot of what appeared to be homeless and strange people. Kate felt on edge and was happy to have Colby right next to her.

Perhaps the prettiest among all the buildings on the street was the Facoltà di Giurisprudenza, Faculty of Law, which occupied a renaissance palazzo with a beautiful inner courtyard. Colby had to use a keycard to get them inside the actual building. Kate was glad to find the graffiti didn't extend inside.

They stopped at Gelateria Gianni, which reminded Kate they needed to talk to Colby and tell him about their plans to go to Venice tomorrow. It also reminded her about the guys they promised to meet up with. She fell back and snagged hold of Ellie, pulling her away from Belgium. "The guys."

"What guys?"

"The guys we're supposed to go out with tomorrow." Maybe this was her way out of the date.

Ellie kissy-faced her response. "If we go early enough, we can be back in time to still go out with them."

"You think?"

"Sure. Venice is only a few hours away. We can even do the whole tourist thing and be back well before seven."

"Okay." Kate looked ahead for Colby. "We need to tell Colby." They hurried to catch up with him.

"Colby, we're going to Venice tomorrow," Kate announced.

He stopped walking. "Venice?"

Ellie interrupted. "Kate's locket was made there."

"Ellie has this crazy idea that the son of the guy who made it will remember Carmela."

"Just because the locket was made there, doesn't mean her mom got it there." Colby sounded skeptical.

"I know." Ellie huffed. "But chances are high because they only sold these lockets from that particular store and there were not a lot made." Ellie's shoulders were square, like she was settling in to argue with him until he gave up.

"Maybe they received it as a gift."

"I hadn't thought of that," Ellie said. Kate hadn't either, but she said nothing. "It doesn't really matter, Colby. It's a lead we have to follow. If it turns out to be nothing, then we at least got to see Venice."

"You shouldn't go alone. Mom and Dad wouldn't like it and Kate, your parents would freak if they knew you were leaving here to search for your birth mother."

He was right. "You can come with us." Kate pushed her shoulders up and grimaced. Colby being there would go a long way in assuaging her fear.

"I can't. I have classes and labs, remember? Just forget about it. You have the address of the shop?"

They nodded.

"Write them a letter. You'll get the same information, but won't have to travel there and you won't be in any danger."

Kate kind of liked Colby's suggestion, but the look on Ellie's face told Kate she better not interfere.

"Look, Colby," Ellie said. "We aren't asking your permission. I'll tell Mom and Kate will tell her parents. We are going."

"Mom and Dad will never let you."

"I'll text them right now. You know they'll let me. You're just blowing smoke."

Colby rolled his eyes and they started walking again. "Why do you two have to go looking for trouble all the time? Kate, just stay here where you are safe."

Kate felt a yank on her bag and turned to see a guy's hand on it. Without a thought, her defense training kicked in and she smacked the guy in the face with the heel of her hand and then kneed him in the groin. He scrambled up, wailing in pain, and took off.

Colby started off after the guy.

"No, Colby. Stop."

He did and stared at Kate.

"Wow, ninja girl. That was amazing." Ellie put her hand up for a high-five and Kate slapped it, adrenaline still rushing through her.

"All those hours in my self-defense classes are finally getting some use." Her face burned. It shocked her that her body had reacted so naturally to the threat.

"I'd say. That was pretty hot actually." Colby grinned.

Ellie cleared her throat. "So, big brother, as you can see, we can take care of ourselves." She put an arm around Kate's shoulder.

Colby raised one eyebrow. "I don't want you two getting hurt. That's all." His eyes seemed to be piercing Kate's.

"We'll be careful. Don't worry." Ellie hugged Colby. "I love you and I'm glad you worry about me, but I'm a big girl. We are big girls. Besides weren't you the one preaching that Kate should explore her *Italian-ness*?"

He glanced at Kate. "Italian-ness, not track down her birth mother. And I can see that you two aren't weak, well at least Kate isn't," he raised an eyebrow and moved out of the way of Ellie's punch. "But don't expect me to be happy about it. And if Mom and Dad say no, I can't let you go."

Ellie pulled out her phone and started texting. Kate palmed her phone in her pocket. She wouldn't text her parents. She'd call them as soon as they got to the party. She didn't think they'd get upset, but she wasn't sure how they'd feel about the search for Carmela in Venice. She hoped they wouldn't forbid her from going since Colby wouldn't be there. Even though she felt a little sick about telling them, she knew she had to. She'd promised to keep them abreast of what she was doing. This was not something she could keep from them, like it or not. At least she could delay telling them.

"And by the way," Colby said. "I'm learning all kinds of interesting stuff about people's tendencies and what they do in certain circumstances when seen through genes. Very fascinating. It's a wonder anyone thinks they have any individual choices at all."

Kate didn't know what to think about that.

"And you, Kate, would be a very interesting test subject for the study." Was this why he'd been so protective of her? He wanted her to be a part of his experiment?

"No thanks. I don't like to be examined and I truly believe I have choices. I don't do things because I've been pre-programmed to do them."

"Think what you will. If you change your mind, I have a questionnaire I could give you."

Kate didn't respond.

"Uh, it's *Feierabend*, everyone. No more school talk. It's party time," Germany said, as they walked through colorful halls and beautiful porticoes as well as sections of buildings adorned with mosaics. Kate examined everything with awe as she did her best not to be left behind.

Finally, they arrived at the party. It was being held at a large house that had been sectioned off into three apartments. The interior was packed with people. They literally had to push their way through the crowds, sweaty bodies hindering their path until they got to the back of the house. She'd been crazy to think she would be able to have a conversation with her parents there. A bartender stood at his bar serving beer but also mineral water, soda, and wine. It seemed most people had wine glasses in their hands. The boys headed straight for the alcohol. Colby stayed back, his eyes perusing the crowds.

"You going to be okay?"

"Of course," Ellie said. "Go. Have fun."

The backyard was a gem. It was large, with grass, fountains and little sections that were secluded from the rest creating private spaces to hide away with someone special. Tables with chairs dotted the garden. The atmosphere was inviting and somehow calm despite the crowds. Music played and people danced, but there wasn't the loud, booming bass or frenzied movements that seemed to prevail at parties in Texas. And everyone was dressed to the nines, glamorous and gorgeous. Kate felt a surge of happiness that they'd bought new clothes. She didn't feel like an American, standing out for everyone to gawk at, and she could find somewhere to call her parents back there, she was sure of it.

However, there were some people who looked oddly familiar. She tried not to let it freak her out, but she found herself ducking away from the glances of certain individuals. These people were Italians and the only other Italians she knew had been in Jersey. She justified ignoring her feelings with the idea that she was thinking they looked familiar simply because they were Italian, nothing more.

That's when she saw him.

11

Martino stood only twenty feet away. He looked amazing. Tall, lean, and ever so handsome. And standing next to him were Constantin and several of the other guys from Admire Piazza Maggiore. They'd also changed and were surrounded by women. Italian women. Kate leaned into Ellie and said, "Look who's here."

She took one look and said, "We are going over there to claim them."

"Claim them? Please. We don't own them."

"But they're going out with us tomorrow."

"That doesn't mean we have any rights to them tonight. How about we observe them. Stay in the shadows and see what kind of guys they are. Maybe we don't want to hurry back from Venice."

Ellie gave Kate a look of complete disbelief. "I don't care how they act tonight. I am gonna get me some action with Constantin tomorrow no matter what."

Kate laughed, but she didn't feel amused. "Fine, but let them come to us. Let's pretend we didn't see them." Kate was sure that when faced with the choice of those women or Ellie and Kate, they would choose the former every time. And she found she didn't really care. Her heart was with another boy. One in Jersey. One she'd never be with again.

"For a while, but…"

And as if Fate was stepping in, a couple of guys walked right up to them. They said something in Italian. Kate smiled. These outfits were doing their job. "We don't speak Italian. Do you speak English by chance?"

"*Sì!* Yes." The guy looked at Kate and said, "But you look Italian."

"Thank you," both Ellie and Kate said.

"What was it you asked?"

"Dance?" Both guys held out their hands. Ellie's eyes sparkled as she moved toward the other guy and took his hand.

"I'm Kate."

"I'm Marco."

"Nice to meet you, Marco. I'd love to dance." She took his hand and they met Ellie and her guy on the dance floor.

Marco and Kate tried hard to have a conversation about something substantial, but the language barrier proved the death of their time together. Ellie didn't seem to care and held on to her dance partner like he was the last man on earth. Kate got a drink and stood by a tall table and people watched. A couple of guys brought her glasses of wine and when she turned them down, they didn't stay for long. Except for one.

"But you're at a party. Certainly you didn't expect to get away from here alcohol free." He gave her half a smile. Definitely a player and not Italian. He'd be singing a different tune if he knew she was still in high school. At least she hoped he would.

"I did. I'm only visiting and I don't want to miss a thing in an alcohol stupor."

"No one said anything about getting drunk."

Kate lifted an eyebrow.

"What I mean is, just let yourself get to the point where you feel good and stop. We could share a taxi."

"Not tonight. Thanks, though. And for the record, I feel great already." And she did. She felt relaxed and was truly enjoying herself.

"Just one glass." He was a persistent bugger.

Kate shook her head and finally, after several more short arguments, he left her alone. She couldn't help but notice how comfortable everyone looked despite their semi-formal dress. They were obviously used to dressing like this for parties. The guys all looked awesome in their button up shirts and jackets. Not a one wore jeans. Perhaps that was why no one was totally out of control on the dance floor or elsewhere. She loved the atmosphere and even found the choppy, Italian-English conversations she had with everyone totally fun.

Someone came up to her and whispered in her ear. Martino's familiar voice filled her mind. "Looks like you got the memo on rule number seven: Dress to kill. Always."

Kate turned her head to look at Martino and laughed. "Actually, that was number ten, right after number nine: Italians love to give constructive criticism. And if you ask advice about buying clothes to fit in as an Italian, you should be prepared to receive advice about everything else."

He chuckled and joined her at the table. "Having a good time?"

"Yes."

"So, this party was your plan for tonight?"

"Yes and we had dinner with friends."

"I couldn't believe it when I saw you standing there alone. Why aren't you on the dance floor with the hottest guy here?"

"Because the hottest guy is standing next to me." She was flirting and she wasn't sure why. This guy was just a lot of fun.

He smiled and looked at her glass, the contents almost gone. "Mineral Water?"

She nodded.

"You don't drink?" He put his beer up to his lips.

"Not here. I don't want to miss anything by getting into a drunken stupor." She was being coy. But he didn't have to know that. She never drank alcohol.

"But you're at a party." He took another long swig of his drink.

"Yes, and I'm having a great time." If he was going to start pressuring her to drink, she was going to have to leave him.

"This is a new concept for me."

"I don't mind if *you* drink."

"You don't drink and you don't dance?"

"I've been dancing, I was taking a break."

"You ready to go again?"

She grinned. "I am." How she loved to dance.

He took her hand.

"Why is your English so good?" She asked before they could start dancing.

"Growing up, I spent most of my summers in America."

She nodded and they started to dance. It was one of those songs that was in-between a fast song and a slow one. He chose to pull her close and opted for a slow dance.

"All summer, huh? Lucky." That was interesting.

"Yep. Sometimes, but when you are learning the family business, it can get trying. If it were all fun and games it would have been different. So you're on vacation, not going to school?"

"Yeah. We leave Sunday."

"Well, I guess you want to squeeze in as much fun as possible before then."

"No worries there. You promised me a great time tomorrow."

"And I will deliver on that promise."

"I have no doubt." She couldn't decide if she should tell him about Venice tomorrow. She decided not to when a fleeting thought that he might invite himself popped into her brain.

He stopped moving.

"Shall we?" He indicated the table they'd come from with a flick of his head. She looked around and realized the floor was empty. Heat spread up her neck and a nervous chuckle escaped her lips. "Guess the music ended?"

"A while ago, actually. It will start up again in ten."

She stepped away from him and gave him a soft punch on his solid arm. "How embarrassing."

"I'm not embarrassed and look around. No one cares. You shouldn't either."

She huffed, not wanting to glance around and see if he was telling the truth. Then she heard a laugh that brought her straight back to Jersey. She scanned the area, but couldn't find where the laugh came from. She was losing it, seriously. She pushed the thought out of her head. But she heard the laughter again and jerked her head in the direction it had come from. Spiders crawled just under her skin. It couldn't be. She was being ridiculous. Veronica couldn't be there. She was in Jersey. But that laugh, it was so distinctive.

"Fine," Kate said, turning to head off, but she stopped in her tracks, her jaw going slack. Martino turned back to see Kate frozen.

"Kate?" he asked and when she didn't move, he followed her gaze to the table next to theirs as a couple of guys left it.

"Veronica? Do you know Veronica from the States?"

Kate shook her head, voices in her head screaming for her to run far away as fast as she could, but her body refusing motion.

He looked back to the crowds. "You're going to have to direct me a bit here. It looks to me like you are looking at Veronica. Let's go over and say hi." Kate snapped out of it and smiled at him.

"No. I can't, sorry." Red hot lava seemed to fill her veins. Veronica was here. Kate glanced back at her and started to move to the opposite end of the gardens but Martino stopped her.

"What's going on?

"I need to find Ellie." She whipped her head around, but couldn't see her or Colby anywhere. She glanced back at Veronica.

Martino took her hand. "Something is obviously up. Tell me. Does it have to do with Veronica? You keep looking at her."

"No."

"She can be a bit nuts sometimes, but she's good at heart, really. If something happened, maybe I can help you two get over it."

He was acting like he knew Veronica well. If he did, Kate needed to

96

get out of there, fast.

"It's not her." She tried to laugh it off to get him off her trail. "I'm just not feeling very well. I'm sorry. I'm sure it's jet lag. We only got in this morning."

"Seriously? Wow. I can't believe you're still awake. I can never make it so late when I come back from Jersey. I crash by five."

Kate's heart thudded hard in her chest. This guy traveled to Jersey every summer to learn the family business. He was friends with Veronica, who was a Marconi. He must be a Marconi as well.

"Can I get you back to your hotel?"

Kate's voice cracked as she spoke. Of course he'd assume she was staying at a hotel. "That's so nice, but I'll find my friends and have them take me. I'll see you tomorrow." She gave him a big smile and pulled away.

"Sleep well," he said.

"I will, I'm sure." She tried hard not to appear frantic as she searched for anyone in her group. If they'd gone inside, she might never find them. Even if she could find her way back to the apartment, she didn't have a key and she'd have to walk alone through the scary part of the campus. No. She had to find Ellie and Colby. She walked around looking with no success, so she found a bench and stood on it. She spotted Ellie first, snuggled next to an evergreen with a guy, kissing. Kate wasn't excited about breaking up their moment, but she had no choice. She had to get out of there. If Veronica saw her it would be over and she'd end up back in Jersey.

Who was she kidding? They'd never let her live after what she'd done.

Kate tried the subtle approach, tapping Ellie on the arm. Ellie didn't respond. Not too much of a shock considering how many people had likely bumped into them. "Ellie," Kate said, grabbing her arm. Ellie grunted but didn't turn. Kate pulled on Ellie's arm and said, "Ellie!" in a harsher tone.

Without turning to Kate, Ellie said, "What, Kate. I'm busy."

"We have to go." Kate looked at the guy and said, "Sorry, she has to go."

"No wait!" Ellie said. Her head turned to Kate and she started to say one thing, but stopped and seemed to decide to say something totally different. "What's going on? You're pale."

Kate flicked a look at the guy Ellie was with and then said, "I'm telling you, we need to leave." Kate smiled up at the guy.

"Can you give me more time? I'd *really* like to stay."

"I get it." Kate grabbed Ellie by the arm and pulled her unceremoniously to the side and whispered in her ear. "Veronica is here."

Ellie wrinkled her brow. "Veronica?"

"You know, the girl who taught me how to be a club girl in Jersey." Kate opened her eyes wide for emphasis and Ellie's shot wide too.

"Seriously? What is she doing here?"

"No idea. Vacation, maybe? You think the mafia gives people vacation time?" Kate wrung her hands. "Come on. Let's get Colby." The music started up again.

"Are you sure? It's not one of your imaginings is it?"

"No. She's here. Colby. Now."

"He's not going to be happy."

"I'm sorry. I know I'm ruining the night for both of you." Kate made a strangled noise.

"You are more important than a mack sesh with a mega hot Italian guy." She sighed. "Slightly, but still." Ellie turned to the Italian guy and said, "Sorry, I have to go. I think you are awesome."

The guy smiled and walked away, obviously happy with Ellie's performance. The dance floor had filled back up and the girls searched and searched until finally they found Colby. "You stay hidden here and I'll go get him. When you see us walking toward the house, head that way."

"Okay." Kate pushed herself into the little nook Ellie had vacated and kept her eyes trained on Ellie as she headed for Colby.

A new song began to play and the number of people dancing suddenly doubled. Kate immediately lost sight of both Ellie and Colby. That's when she thought she saw more people that she recognized from Jersey. She shook her head and closed her eyes. When she opened them again, she recognized more and more people. She had to get out of there and fast. She stepped out of her hidey-hole and right into none other than Veronica.

12

"Well looky here!" Veronica said, her predatory eyes fixed on Kate. Kate's self-defense instruction was stuck in her brain. The file would not open. This was it. It was over. Her body had turned to ice. Veronica had her.

"I'm glad to see that I'm not the only one who has to suffer."

Kate's eyes shifted around for an escape route, but her body still couldn't move.

"Looks like you haven't changed a bit. Still afraid of me, are you? I taught you better than that. Snap out of it, Kate." Veronica sneered.

And she did.

Veronica wasn't after her. She wasn't even surprised to find her.

"What's puzzling me is that you are here and not in Venice." Her lip curled in disgust.

Kate pulled on a tiny thread of courage in her gut and said, "Well, you know how that goes. Believe me, I'd rather be in Venice." Heat filled her belly. Veronica thought she should be in Venice. Interesting. Even though she felt less shaken now, her heart still ran its fastest race yet.

"Yeah. Men should never be in charge of big stuff like this."

Kate nodded and then Veronica put on her ugly face again as if she just remembered she hated Kate.

"Still. I can't seem to catch a break. First they send me here and then I find you here too? I'm going to ask to be transferred."

"Don't do that. I-I-I'm only visiting. I'll be gone tomorrow."

"I-I-I. Good grief. Take a chill pill. Where's your home base?"

"Wouldn't you like to know?"

Veronica stood a little taller and said, "Maybe I would."

"Sorry, we can't always get what we want." It occurred to Kate that all Veronica had to do was say something to one person. One right person who knew about her and she was a goner. She tapped her foot to release some pent up energy.

"Whatever. As long as you're far away from me, I don't care where your sorry butt is." She gave Kate a withering gaze. "One thing's for sure, I'm outta here. *Ciao!*" She stormed away, heading straight for the house, but she didn't get far.

Martino walked up and blocked Veronica's path. "You two do know each other. I knew it."

A hot wave of acid blew through Kate's gut and she slouched to squelch the pain.

"That loser?" Veronica said. "I've already forgotten her." She sneered and tried to push past Martino, who continued to prevent it.

"Come on. Whatever bad blood there is between you, you can get rid of it."

"Get out of my way, Martino, and if it's your M.O to hang with Bellinis now, then I don't need you in my life. Move." Her words and command sent chills up Kate's spine and she turned to take off, keeping one eye on Veronica. Nothing good could come of this. Veronica ducked and went under Martino's frozen arm and then gave a gesture no one could deny was the ultimate in rudeness.

Kate rushed down the narrow trail only to feel a hand clamp onto her upper arm and stop her progress. She pulled, not wanting to face Martino, but he was too strong and kept her there.

"Bellini?" he said to her back. Maybe he'd let her go if she didn't turn around. She pulled again, still unable to conjure up any of the moves she'd learned in self-defense. He did not let her go, but he didn't say anything else either.

She closed her eyes, took a deep breath through her nose before turning to face him, exhaling as she did. He let go, and shoved his hands into his pockets.

She didn't speak. He didn't either, but he raised an eyebrow. The question was undeniable, but she didn't know how to answer it. She couldn't tell him she was a Bellini, it would be a sure-fire way to speed up her death. Her brain churned, trying to uncover a solution. She could turn and run. She didn't owe him anything. But if she did that, it would make him seek answers through Veronica. She'd rather put her spin on things.

"Okay. I lied. I do know Veronica. I met her in Jersey and let's just say it didn't go well."

"Because you're a Bellini?"

"Maybe. I'm not sure. She never explained why she had an immediate dislike of me." She didn't want to say the words, but felt them slip out of her mouth anyway. "So, you're a Marconi? Martino Marconi?"

He shook his head and said, "No."

She pressed her eyebrows together. "No?"

"I'm a Gatti." Now that was a name she hadn't even heard while in Jersey. She forced her face not to show it.

"Oh." What next? What should she say? She had no clue.

"I know there are a lot of you, but why haven't I ever met you before?" His face softened with curiosity.

"I'm not in Jersey often," she hedged.

Now he furrowed his brow and shifted on his feet. "Why not?"

Her mouth went dry and she swallowed hard. An idea found its way into her mind. She clutched her hands in front of her and forced herself to relax. "Can we just forget about our last names and be friends? Seriously. I stay away from Jersey so that I don't have to get into it, ya know?"

He appeared to be thinking and she let him. Her stomach roiled and her heart pounded in her chest. She had to force herself not to bolt.

People snaked around and between them and it didn't take long for them to inch over to the bushes.

"While I agree about the name thing, I think you're keeping something else from me."

She didn't speak. He did.

"I hate that lines are drawn in the sand simply because we belong to one family or the other, but there are reasons for that. Reasons that have been in play for many years."

"I didn't think I'd have to worry about it here in Italy."

He chuckled. "Yeah, right."

She wasn't sure how to take that. Was he being funny or sarcastic?

"Look, I didn't know your last name and you didn't know mine and we got along just fine. Don't let something Veronica said change that. Can't we pretend we are Martino and Kate and nothing more?"

He shifted on his feet again. The Gattis must have had a real beef with the Bellinis. She wouldn't ask why. Not now.

"Maybe."

She huffed. "Why maybe? Let's just agree and make it happen." She knew she was on thin ice, but this whole family against family thing was grating on her nerves all of a sudden.

"Look. I said maybe."

She pressed her lips into a thin line. "Whatever." She turned to go. Exactly what she wanted to happen was happening. She hated to think she had Veronica to thank for it. But he grabbed her hand. "No one can know who you are."

Kate frowned. He didn't say what she thought he had, did he? "Well, I think the cat's out of the bag already."

"What do you mean?"

Kate let out an exasperated sound. "Veronica. She won't keep that little nugget quiet."

"True, but I meant with my family. Tomorrow at dinner, no one can know you are a Bellini."

A tingle raced through her. He still wanted to have dinner with her. He was trying to figure out how to make it work. "Oh. Got it." It seemed strange that he would want to risk everything to take her to that dinner. Who she was wouldn't stay hidden forever. There was always the off chance that his parents had known hers and would see the resemblance to her mother or father. A volcano stirred in her gut.

He tapped his index finger on his lips and narrowed his eyes as he thought. All she wanted to do was get the heck out of there, but she'd wait for him to make the decision he was obviously very conflicted about. She saw the decision form in his eyes. "You're right. It shouldn't matter. But, the truth is that it does, so we'll keep it a secret tomorrow. Veronica won't be anywhere near, but I think we should change your name."

"Huh?"

"Well, if someone from my family mentions you or your friend by name to Veronica, we don't want to give her any reason to believe it's you. So, what name have you always wished was yours?"

"Uh," she stammered.

"How about Cara?"

"Okay." She had lost control of the situation. There would be no getting out of the dinner.

"Cara Mancini." He gave a curt nod. "Yes. That's it. A fine Italian name with no mafia connection."

Kate couldn't help herself. She laughed. An uncomfortable sound ricocheting off the space between them.

He took a step closer to her. "It is absurd, isn't it?"

Kate continued to laugh and he took another step toward her. "I'm so glad we worked this out today and not at dinner tomorrow." Worry flooded Kate again. She could only hope he'd keep her identity a secret forever.

Waving hands at the opposite end of the pathway grabbed her attention. Ellie saw Kate see her and stopped waving. Colby stood beside her. Kate's worry faded, just like that.

"Okay then, tomorrow?" Maybe they would end up staying longer in Venice and have to call the guys to give them the bad news.

"Or you could stay now that Veronica is gone." Martino spoke in low, soft tones.

Kate glanced behind him. He turned to look. "Actually, my friends are ready to go. Sorry."

"Fine." He leaned down and kissed her on both cheeks. Despite her desire never to see him again, his kisses seemed to burn into her skin, a traitorous physical reaction. "Tomorrow it is."

She walked past him to Ellie and Colby, their eyes focused on him the whole time.

"What was that all about?" Ellie asked.

"I'll tell you once we get out of here." A terrible sense of foreboding hit her.

"So, show us where she is," Colby said.

"She left." It seemed now she had bigger issues.

Colby's eyes darted to the dance floor, no doubt looking for the girl he'd been forced to leave.

"But not before she had a chance to run into me and give me a shakedown."

"She talked to you?" Colby moved in close, taking one of her hands in his.

Kate nodded. "Yeah. We need to get out of here and fast. Martino knows I'm a Bellini now, too." She didn't want to tell them she thought she'd seen other people from the club too. She wasn't really sure about that and didn't want to cause more alarm.

"No way." Colby frowned, obviously upset.

"I'm sorry for ruining your night, Colby."

His eyes brightened and he smiled before putting his arm around Kate. "It's not your fault. You're way more important than this party. You're nuts if you think I wouldn't choose you over this."

Once they made it through the house and were well on their way back to the apartment, Colby glanced around and then said, "Tell me what she said."

"It was weird. She said something about them sending me here too. It was like she had no idea what happened to me. Like she thought I was still in Jersey."

"Serious?"

"Yes. She didn't know I escaped."

"Someone sent her here?"

"Yeah. And she was mad I was here. Thought I should be somewhere else."

"Where? And who sent her? Why?" They kept a brisk pace down the sidewalk.

Kate didn't want to say where since it was Venice. She'd tell Ellie later. "Does it matter? She was sent here for some reason and thought I had been too. Maybe she got into trouble or something. The worst part, I think, is Martino knows I'm a Bellini. He's a Gatti, but apparently they are thick as thieves with the Marconis. It took him some serious reflection to decide I wasn't a bug he needed to squash."

"Maybe we should go to Venice right now." Ellie screwed up her face. "It's getting too dangerous for you to be here."

Colby sighed. "In the middle of the night? I don't think so. And what? A Gatti? Martino has something to do with this?"

"Tomorrow will be okay. We'll go early like we planned." Kate stepped around an abandoned box on the sidewalk. "Gatti is another mafia family, I guess." She tried to say it without letting the concern she felt bleed out.

"It's crazy that you befriended some random guy and he's linked to Jersey. I think you two should fly out tomorrow. What did Mom and Dad say?" Colby turned to Ellie.

"They told me to have a good time." She smirked. "And we can't stay here. Hello! Scary Creepy Girl is here. And Martino knows." Kate's gut twisted. She hadn't contacted her parents yet. She needed to do that and quick. She pulled out her phone.

"And you're sure she's here. You aren't just imagining it because of your dreams? Scary dreams can totally play with your mind." Colby's eyes bored into Kate.

"Veronica is not imaginary. Totally real." Thinking about just how real she was made Kate's chest squeeze.

"You should take the driver to Venice." They turned down the street the apartment was on.

"No, that takes an extra hour. We'll take the train." Ellie scowled.

Kate started a text to her mom knowing it was about the time she would be waking up.

Kate: Hi, Mom and Dad. We are heading in for the night. We got to see so many cool things. Attaching pictures.

She picked out her ten favorite pictures from the day and attached them. The ball was in her mom's and dad's courts now. Kate would tell them more after they texted back. She made sure her phone was on vibrate and then shoved it into her bag. She had this strange sensation she was being watched.

"What if Veronica is going to take the train somewhere tomorrow morning?" Colby was shaking his head. "There are too many variables in this equation."

Kate shushed him. "Let's keep our voices down."

"She's not going to Venice. It's going to be okay. Relax. Kate's safer anywhere but here." Ellie kicked at a small rock in her path and it skittered into the street. "And Jersey," she added under her breath.

Kate could tell Colby was still worried, his lips were pressed into a thin line and he was opening and closing his fists. "But, what if you get there and do find your birth mother and it puts you in danger again?"

"We're banking on Carmela being the good one in the family. You know, because Kate is so good." Ellie gave Colby a look that said, *Hello, catch up. You're going to freak Kate out.*

Kate couldn't concentrate on what they were talking about. She couldn't shake the feeling that someone was there, in the dark. Colby stopped walking and took Kate's arm, choosing to ignore Ellie. "Well, either way I don't like the idea. It could lead you to a terrible emotional place. I don't want to see you get hurt by your birth parents any more than you already have been."

"I'll be okay," Kate said, not sure it was true. She started walking again. "And maybe, if I can't find Carmela, I can find her parents. My maternal grandparents. I can find out who my other relatives are—on my birth mother's side. They must be good. They have to be good." Deep down Kate wanted something to give her license to be good, to be the person she believed and hoped she was.

"It would be interesting to find them and see if they are good." Colby's scientific mind had set in, overtaking any emotional attachment he had to Kate.

"Maybe you'll find your lineage goes to a king or queen or emperor. Something cool like that." Ellie's eyes sparkled in the lamplight as they passed under it.

"That would be cool to find out." They reached the apartment, but Kate didn't stop. Instead, she whispered, "Let's keep going, you guys, just in case we were followed."

Ellie started to crane her neck around. Kate grabbed her arm. "Don't look back. Just keep walking." Sweat started to pool on her forehead. "Uh, where are we going to go?"

"I don't know. Ideas? Are you guys sensing anyone?"

"No," they said in unison.

"We could always call Devlin."

"And have him do what? Drive us around all night?"

"He could drop us off at a hotel and then we could get a taxi to pick us up or something. Whoever is on our tail is on foot. It wouldn't be difficult to lose them."

"Alright." Colby huffed and pulled out his phone.

Devlin picked them up ten minutes later and dropped them off at a nice hotel and restaurant nearby. They sat on some sofas in the lounge area, the receptionist giving them nasty looks every time they happened to look her way. Kate pulled out her phone and found she'd received two texts.

Dad: Sounds like you've been busy. What's up for tomorrow? I'm headed to work, so I won't text you right back. Your mom just left to take a neighbor to the doctor. She's got a busy day planned. Keep us informed.

Kate: We are going to Venice for a day trip early tomorrow. Ellie is totally excited to ride in the gondolas. I'll tell you all about it as the day goes on. I'm so tired. We are going to bed. Have fun today.

The second text was from Johansen.

Johansen: Hello. Italy. The mafia. You are a mafia child on the run.

She'd gotten the text almost an hour ago.

Kate: But, the same mafia isn't in Italy, is it?

They waited twenty minutes before calling a random cab to take them back to the apartment, and hurried inside as soon as they arrived. The other boys weren't back yet. Kate kept checking her phone, but did not get any other texts

"I don't like this at all," Colby said. "Not at all."

"Yeah. I'm kinda freaking out too. Tomorrow won't get here fast enough."

"You two should go home on the first flight out. I'm not kidding."

"No," Ellie said. "We are not going to let them intimidate us."

"Good grief, Ellie. Are you hearing yourself?"

Kate didn't want them to fight. She put an end to it. "We need to get out of here. That is a given. Let's compromise, Ellie. We are going to go to Venice in the morning then we fly out from an airport nearby."

Colby huffed. He still didn't like it. Kate needed a change of subject.

"So, tell us about the study you guys are working on. Have you been able to prove genes and DNA determine everything you do?"

"We're working on it." His eyes brightened. "You seriously should be a part of this study. It would be fascinating to include you and your history."

"I already said no to that." Kate slipped off her shoes and dangled them from her fingers.

"You could see what kind of people you come from." Colby raised his eyebrows, offering her a questioning gaze.

The Bellini bosses and Vincenzo flashed through her mind. She knew about half of her relatives. That was more than she ever wanted to know of her birth father's family. She swung her shoes and frowned.

Ellie joined in. "Was your family full of paupers or servants or were they the ones in charge?" She wrestled her feet out of her shoes and left them by the door. "I think it would say a lot about a family if they were paupers back then and clawed their way to prosperity today. Heck! I want to know where I come from." Ellie spun around. "I mean, I know England, but what kind of people were our ancestors?"

That did sound fun to explore to Kate, but she was a bit scared too. "I can see researching that in the States, in English, but how would I even go about finding the information here when I don't know Italian?"

"I'm sure someone will know. We'll ask the jeweler in Venice to lead us to the right place."

"Make a copy of everything you find for me, okay?" Colby said. He'd totally forgotten his objections to their going to Venice. Or perhaps he knew it was a futile fight.

"Okay," Ellie said.

"You too, Kate."

"I told you. I don't want to be a part of the study."

Colby sighed.

Kate's eyes felt heavy despite her whirring mind and the recent scare she'd experienced. "I'm going to bed. I'm dead, and six will come too early for sure." She hoped she'd be able to sleep despite the unsettled churning in her gut.

"Now that you mention it, I'm pretty tired myself." Ellie followed Kate into their room. She stopped right as she hit the door. "If you want to go back to the party, Colby, feel free."

They never heard him leave.

Once Kate and Ellie were in their beds, Kate said, "Ellie, listen."

"Uh-huh," she said, obviously already getting comfy enough to sleep.

"Venice."

"I know," Ellie said through a yawn. "It's going to be awesome. I can't wait to see all the cool bridges and stuff."

Kate swallowed hard. "No. Veronica thought I should be in Venice."

Ellie shifted on the bed, cradling her head in one palm, her elbow buried into the bedding, supporting it. "So you did know. You lied, Kate Hamilton."

"I know. I didn't want Colby to freak out even more about us going." She had other secrets too. Bigger, more terrible secrets.

"Yeah. He'd never let us go if he knew."

"I don't think we should go." Kate's heart thundered.

"What?" Ellie sat up. Kate could see her silhouette against the moonlight coming in from the window.

"Keep your voice down." Kate whispered. "Listen, I didn't only not want Colby to freak, I also needed some time to think. It's too dangerous for us to stay here—at least for me. And while I don't know why Veronica thought I should be in Venice, I think that's enough to tell us we shouldn't go. I'm going to get on the first flight back in the morning. I want you to—"

"No." Ellie interrupted. "I won't accept that. We are going to Venice, talking to the jeweler and then and only then, are we flying home."

"Ellie. Be reasonable. I refuse to put you in danger."

"I am being reasonable. I will not let that little witch keep us from finding your mom just because she thought you should be in Venice. And I understand there are risks. Like I told Colby. We are big girls and can take care of ourselves. We know there is the chance of trouble and will watch for it. We can't let fear run our lives."

"If anything happens to you, Ellie, I don't know—"

"Nothing is going to happen. And just so you know, I'll happily put myself in danger for you."

"Don't say that!"

Ellie cleared her throat loudly. She'd had enough. "So, tell me about Martino." She squealed. "I was going to wait until the train ride, but I don't think I'm going to be sleeping just yet." Ellie climbed onto the floor and squeezed in next to Kate. Kate sighed in defeat and gave her the blow by blow account.

13

She wasn't sure if it was the fact that nightmares had kept her from sleep most of the night, the rocking and consistent hum of the train, or just relief to finally be leaving Bologna, but Kate fell asleep seconds after the train left the station. She slept hard for the hour and a half it took to travel to Venice, and Ellie woke her when they were about to pull up to the station. Kate stretched her arms toward the ceiling and grunted. "That felt great. No nightmares."

The look of determination that had dominated Ellie's face since she talked Kate into going to Venice last night was gone.

"Whoa! I'm guessing you didn't sleep as well as I did." Kate yawned, her hand covering her mouth.

"Are you sure you want to look for Carmela? You called out like three times last night and once while here on the train. You did have at least one nightmare. Maybe it wasn't a good idea to pursue this."

"You can't be serious."

"I know I pushed you into this and I know we're almost there, but maybe we should stay on the train, not go to Venice, but to the airport and fly back home."

"Yes, I had some pretty bad dreams last night, but I had no idea I did on the train. I feel like I slept great this past couple of hours. That said, I think the nightmares will continue until I get my answers. I want the dreams to stop and I think Venice has a good chance of making that happen." Something fluttered low in her gut.

"Are you ready for what you're going to find? What if you don't get answers?"

"Yes. I'm ready for what I do or don't find. Either way, it puts an end to the questions." Kate pulled out a mirror and fiddled with her hair. She swallowed hard, trying to get some moisture back into her mouth. "I can't shake the feeling that it's the questions that are fueling the dreams."

Ellie slid over and fixed a few strands of Kate's hair before going to work on her own. "Okay then I'm on board, too. As long as you don't get shot at or kidnapped."

Kate gave her a disapproving look then sat up straight. "Let's not even consider that. Blinders, Ellie. Blinders."

"Okay. It's going to be creepy being here, though, knowing that all of those mafia people were spawned here."

"Only the originals," Kate wasn't sure if she was reassuring herself or Ellie. "Their children were spawned in the good old U.S. of A." She pulled out her phone. One text from Johansen. Nothing from her mom. Either she was okay with them traveling to Venice or she hadn't gotten the message yet.

Johansen: Of course they are the same. They don't want us to know that, but yes. New Jersey mafia and the Italian mafia are one in the same. Don't stand out. I'm doing some research on the families and where they are headquartered in Italy so you can avoid them. Whatever you do, don't stand out.

Kate: We are in Venice today. We will be careful.

"Truly, there's something about being with a people that produced someone who would even think of creating the mafia. Insane." Ellie gave an exaggerated shudder.

"Yeah and I'm one of them." Kate frowned deeply. "Johansen got back to me. It seems the mafia is alive and well in Italy. He's doing some research for us, so we can avoid the families from New Jersey while here. He doesn't want us to stand out." She wished she'd thought to research the mafia in Italy before they left home.

"First off, there are two kinds of people. Evil and good. You're one of the good ones." Ellie nodded rapidly. "At least you have choices. And don't worry, I'll try not be my normal *loud* self. I'll tone it down."

Kate hoped she had choices.

Ellie would have to go against her nature in order not to stick out. It probably wasn't possible. All Kate could hope for was that no one from the Marconi or Bellini families would be in Venice and notice them.

She looked over the information about the jewelry shop in Venice one more time before they exited the train and left the station, emerging into a humid, but cool morning in Venice.

It was a sight to behold. They stepped out into the crowds of tourists and commuters and Kate pulled up her map of Venice on her phone. The main entrance was packed with tour groups even though it was early and all followed the long roadway along the water. "We need to go this way to find tourist information." She pointed. While Kate didn't mind using her phone to map everything, she didn't want to run out of battery before they headed back home, and she planned to take a lot of pictures, which took a lot of battery power. They would get a physical map from the tourist information center and use it instead.

On their way there, they stopped in front of St. Mark's library, the Biblioteca Nazionale Marciana, a beautiful, majestic building that shone brilliant white in the early morning sun.

"Maybe we should go in here and see if they have a map." Kate stared up at the building, admiring the second floor balcony and sculptures that sat atop the building, above the many columns. "And we could ask about finding our ancestors while we're at it. You'd think a library would have that information. Right? We could kill two birds with one stone."

"Nice thinking. If the information isn't in there," Ellie indicated the library, and started up the steps to the entrance, "we haven't lost anything and can go to the information booth."

Kate and Ellie rushed up the steps only to find the library wasn't open yet. "Well that was easy." They laughed.

"Yep. I'm not waiting half an hour to go in there."

They hurried down the steps and followed the Internet map to tourist information. There was a long line. They stood in St. Mark's Market Square or Piazza. She'd thought the Piazza in Bologna had been large, but this was at least twice as big. St. Mark's Basilica stood at the opposite end of the open, cobbled space and was enormous. It was impossible for her eyes not to follow the church's bell tower to its heights. It was surrounded by what appeared to be government buildings, restaurants, and shops. Easy to imagine the square being the center of the city for centuries. The absence of pigeons and birds that seemed to dominate the Bologna Piazza was a curiosity.

"I don't want to waste a bunch of time in this line. We haven't moved at all yet," Kate said, leaning out of the line to see what was happening at the front.

"Yeah." Ellie commiserated. "Let's go to the jeweler and then come back. This is probably slammed because of all the tourists arriving. I'm sure the line will be shorter later."

They walked all the way to the jeweler's, which was off the beaten path, using the GPS on Kate's phone. Kate said a silent prayer that the jeweler would be open, hoping she wasn't being too unrealistic since it was still early. If worse came to worst, they'd go back to the library and wait outside until it opened or possibly check the line at the tourist information booth again. When they arrived, a man was opening the shop's door.

"*Mi scusi*," Kate said, relieved.

The man turned quickly like they'd startled him. He put his hand to his chest. "*Mi avete spaventato.*"

"Are you opening up?"

"*Si*, but not for an hour."

Both girls sighed, disappointed. Kate's head hung. It was back to St.

Mark's square.

The man pushed open the door and said, "But for you, we are open now." He walked inside and flipped on the lights. The girls followed, a little hesitant. He shut the door behind them, but kept the Closed sign facing out and locked the door from the inside. Kate's heart thumped hard against her chest at the thought of being trapped. She took two deep breaths and the feeling subsided.

"I'm Edmondo. What can I interest you two in this fine morning? Perhaps a nice keepsake of your time in Italy?" He swished his way behind the jewelry counter and began unlocking one of the cabinets. He straightened, pulling out several necklaces and rings. His gaze settled on Kate and then what appeared to be her chest as he set the jewelry on the glass counter.

"Oh, my. I had no idea." He moved from behind the counter and stood in front of Kate. Kate felt really uncomfortable now and started to back up. "Oh, no. I'm sorry. It's just that you have one of my father's lockets." Immediately, Kate's hand flew to the locket and she stared at him.

"He only made twenty of those and only for very special customers. We don't get many tourists seeking us out. He would be so pleased to know someone as lovely as you received one of them and have come to pay your respects."

"So you know all the people who bought them?" Kate clasped her hands in front of her. This was amazing.

"Me? No. But my dad did. He often talked about the people."

Her heart raced. "Did he talk about the people who bought this one?" Kate lifted the locket and tilted her chin back so he could get a better look. A tiny flutter filled her belly.

"If I could get a closer look, I could maybe look up the information."

Kate took off the locket and handed it to him feeling dizzy.

"You have taken such good care of this. It's like it is brand new." Edmondo glanced up and smiled at her.

"I just had it cleaned." Her breath seemed bottled in her chest. Would he know about Carmela?

Edmondo pulled out a familiar tool roll, but Kate stopped him. "If you want to know the number inside, it's twenty."

"Well, that saved us a little effort. Perhaps you'd like to look at these pieces," he indicated the items he'd pulled out earlier, "while I go to the office and check the books." Ellie moved quickly to the counter and picked up a necklace as he disappeared through a door at the side of the store. Kate could tell nothing this store carried would be in her price range. Everything was very fine. It made her proud to think her birth parents had cared about quality when they had chosen the locket.

Ellie modeled the various other jewelry for Kate while Edmondo was gone and it settled Kate's nerves somewhat. "I've got to have this necklace. It's crazy how a gondola crafted by the right person can be elegant." The black onyx gondola hung from a silver chain and had what looked like rubies inset. It was magnificent. "It's the perfect keepsake from this trip. I can't wait to ride on one. We should choose a black gondola."

"I agree." Kate tucked a strand of hair behind her ear chewed lightly on her cheeks.

"What do you think of this one?" Ellie held up a charm bracelet, but before Kate could reply Edmondo returned with a dark brown ledger and flipped through the pages.

"I'm pretty sure the sales record of that beauty is in this book. I think fourteen years ago…"

"Actually, I believe it would have been closer to fifteen or so years."

He nodded and flipped through more pages, finally landing on one particular notation. "Ah, yes. Here it is." He turned the book around so the girls could read the entry his finger sat on. *Vincenzo Bellini for Carmela Bellini* and they had both signed the ledger. Kate ran her fingers over the signatures as if that would somehow transport her back to that day.

"Did your father tell you any stories about this couple?" she pressed.

"The only thing I remember about what he said was that the couple was *shining with happiness*. They had a child, a girl with them."

Kate swallowed hard. Cold prickles shot up her arm.

"My father had been waiting for just the right couple to offer the last locket to and he picked them." As if something suddenly occurred to him, Edmondo frowned. "Wait a minute. You're not...No. You couldn't be. My father said the couple were Italian but lived in America." His eyes brightened and he smiled. "It is you, isn't it? You were the baby."

Kate nodded. He shook his head and then moved right up to her. Kate had to resist the urge to step back. He put his hands on the sides of her face and kissed each of her cheeks. "I'll have you know that my father was not in the jewelry business for money, although he made plenty of that. He considered his pieces works of art and was very choosy about whom he'd allow buy them. Me? I can't be so picky, but I like to honor his memory whenever I see someone with one of his special pieces."

"Do you know anything about their families, then?" Ellie asked.

"If I once did, I don't remember now."

"Were they from here possibly?"

"I seem to remember something about that, but I can't be certain. There's a good chance they had family here. I do remember they lived in the U.S., like I said."

"You've been a great help. Do you mind if I take a picture of the entry in the ledger?"

"Oh, my. Wait," Edmondo said. "Are you saying these two lovely people are no longer?"

Ellie nodded and tears welled in Kate's eyes, not because Kate thought they were dead, but because they were truly dead to her, alive or not.

"Don't cry, my dear. You will be reunited in heaven with them. My father was rarely wrong in his judgment of others and he judged your parents to be—what is that phrase?—the creams of the crop."

"Thank you," Kate squeaked out. She didn't dare tell him it was *cream* and not *creams*.

"Well, Kate was adopted after her parents' demise and she was here hoping to find out if her grandparents are alive, or some aunts, uncles...you know, any relatives. Have an idea where we might start?" Ellie was the best. She was asking the questions Kate was now unable to.

"That is a good question. I'd assume records like that would be kept with state records, the church or the library. We have an amazing library here in town with millions of original documents. Yes. That is where I would start. If they were from here, perhaps you will find birth records there."

"Thank you," Ellie said. "You've been a great help. I really love this necklace," she indicated the black and ruby gondola. "I'd like to buy it."

"Most certainly," Edmondo said and rang her up. Ellie then asked to take his picture and a picture of the interior of the shop.

When the two girls walked out of the store, they heard the click of the lock behind them. Edmondo really had opened just for them. Ellie turned and snapped a picture of the outside of the shop.

"Your parents were here and they were good. I knew it." They walked down a path toward the main square.

"That was nice to hear, but something must've happened to make them bad." Kate tapped her fist against her lips.

"Only Vincenzo and that's debatable. Not Carmela. And I bet you anything they came here to show you off to family and since his family was in Jersey, they came to see Carmela's parents. Your birth grandparents. Here in Venice."

"Or they were just on vacation."

"Another possibility, but I choose to be optimistic." She gave Kate a pointed look. "Let's go to the library and uncover both our heritages and maybe, just maybe, we'll find Carmela in the process; but before we leave, why don't you jot down what you just learned and I'll sketch a picture of this place."

"Sounds good." They sat on the first unoccupied bench they came upon and got to work filling more pages inside Kate's search journal.

14

The girls stood outside the La Biblioteca Nazionale Marciana again and stared up at the ornately carved stone that screamed of the noblest classical style of the Renaissance. It fit in nicely with its Venetian surroundings, with its columns, arches, and statues.

The hopeful ache Kate had buried before coming to Italy was back.

"And I thought the library in New York was cool." Ellie said. "Europeans truly know how to make amazing buildings."

"Right? The buildings are works of art for sure."

"It makes me itch to paint."

"I bet it does. Get good pictures and you'll be able to in only a few days."

"I seriously can't wait." She stomped her foot a few times and let out a high pitched wail. "Does that make me a nerd?"

"Yes!"

Ellie slugged Kate and gave her a nasty look.

"Just kidding, man. You've found your passion, and I think it's normal to yearn for it. And besides, you would never be a nerd. Ever." Kate squeezed Ellie's upper arm.

"You must be my best friend or something." She put her arm around Kate and they spent ten minutes taking picture after picture outside the library. Some were silly with one of them posing all crazy, but the rest were of little things they loved about the building.

"Okay. We've stalled enough. I think it's time to go inside and do what we came to do."

Kate sighed. "Ellie, I'm scared. Really scared. I want to find Carmela so badly, but I don't know if I could take it if we discovered she was scary like Vincenzo."

"I thought we decided Vincenzo was okay, just trapped in that family, a victim of his circumstances. I mean, they wanted to kill his wife and only child. They took everything from him. If you took him out of that life, he would be awesome."

"Yes, but, oh, I don't know. I wish neither one of them were wrapped up in the mafia. If my birth mother was a nark, then that means that she was a part of that life if only for a little while. But, if she worked for the FBI and was inserted into that life, that means she was good to the core, don't you think?"

"You're going to drive yourself crazy if you try to make distinctions like that. It doesn't matter when a person decides to become good, just that they do. And, you'll never know unless you find her. We have to do that first."

"I know." Kate bit her bottom lip and then took a deep breath. "Let's do this."

It was a strange dichotomy walking from the bustling outdoors full of laughter and the raised voices of tour directors, into the quiet, almost silent library. Something gripped at Kate's heart as she entered the building. She couldn't quite tell if it was a warning of danger or some type of an urging to continue, so she continued to see what would come of it.

They'd walked into what appeared to be a museum or a church with paintings and statues, no books. No circulation or information desk. Gold dominated the interior. Even the ceilings and walls were works of art. As they listened to people talking in low voices, they discovered that the library was created to preserve art, written or otherwise. It didn't match their idea of library at all.

As they were about to give up, they finally found the room for scholars and books. It was quite Harry Potterish with rows of long tables to study and little lamps dotting the tables. There were no computers, though. They found a lady sitting at the front of the room who looked official, with a tight bun and a pencil in hand.

"Do you speak English?" Ellie asked.

"*Sì.*" The woman wore a flowing blouse and pencil skirt with comfortable looking sandals. Her blue-rimmed glasses gave her a playful look.

"Hi. We're looking to do some family history. You know, see who my grandparents are and stuff." The woman directed them out of the study area.

"Yes, the civil registry is what you want. It is easily accessed through Family Search. You could go to the government building and get the same information, but I've found Family Search is much faster. You'll need to go to the computer room. It's a bit hard to find." She looked back inside the Harry Potter room they'd just left and then said, "Let me show you the way." She walked with a confident gait and led them to an enclosed area with twenty or so computers, grouped in pairs. She selected one and typed away before turning it over to the girls.

"I've changed the language to English so you'll be able to read the instructions, but the records will be in Italian. I've also pulled up Family Search. If for some reason you lose your way, the address is familysearch.org. If you create an account, you'll be able to track everything you find. Do you want to set one up now?"

The girls glanced at each other. "No," they said in unison. They stood behind the chair the librarian was using.

"Okay. Let's use this dummy account for now. You can always set up an account later."

"What is the deceased's name?" She sat poised to type in the information.

"The deceased?"

"Well, this site won't show you information on the living, only the dead. At least for the most part."

"Oh, sorry. I was hoping to maybe find my grandparents. I hope they're living."

The librarian craned her head back to them. "Do you know their names? If so, we can put them in the Find search and see if they show up. If they do, we will know they are deceased."

"Oh, I don't know their names. I was hoping to find them linked up to my parents."

"Ah. Well, what you're talking about doing is something different than I thought. The search could find them if they are currently alive assuming their birth or christening records have been indexed into Family Search, however you won't be able to see them on a pedigree chart. Which means you won't find them connected to you."

She swiveled in her chair to face them. "Do you at least know where they are from?"

"Here. Venice."

"Ok. You can try to find something here, with the Records button." She clicked the button that said RECORDS.

"You can search the civil records, birth records, death records, and christening records here. If as I said, the records have been indexed. Anything past 1809 *should* show up in here."

"Indexed?"

She smiled. "Well, there's a process for records ending up in this or any other database. First, someone has to find the record. Then they have to record the record, taking a picture or scanning it or something like that. Then, that copy is input into a computer database. At that point, indexers take that information and enter it into a program that makes the information searchable—like first name, last name, etc."

"Oh. I hadn't thought about someone having to get the information that's in here."

The librarian stood up and offered the seat to Kate, who took it. "Yes. Librarians. We know all sorts of fascinating things." She grinned.

"Where does this information come from?" Ellie sat in the chair in front of the computer adjacent to Kate's.

"Lots of places. Church records, state records, headstones, histories."

"You mean like births, baptisms, and stuff."

"*Si*. Marriages, too. Do you know when your parents were married? The approximate year? You can put that information in and see what you get." The watch on the librarian's wrist vibrated.

"I need to go. Explore the site. Get comfortable with it. If you need to print, you may. Donations are appreciated." She pointed to a printer in the corner of the room. A large canister sat beside it with an Italian word written on it. They assumed it said *donations*. "I'll be back as soon as I can." She hurried out of the room.

Kate cleared her throat, her mouth dry, and had a sudden desire to leave the room and get the heck out of the library.

"Go ahead, Kate. Put in your mom's information."

"But."

"No buts. This is it."

Not knowing exactly why, Kate put in her adoptive mom's name instead. Abrie Hamilton. The pictures must have been more important to her at the moment than her birth mother.

"Not her. Your birth mother," Ellie said.

No matches.

Kate put in Tom Hamilton, ignoring Ellie.

No matches.

"What was that about?"

"I don't know. I just thought that maybe…" She still hadn't told Ellie about the pictures. She had to be careful about what she said.

"Your adoptive parents were Italian?"

"My mom, at least. I overheard her reading from an Italian cookbook. In Italian! Fluent Italian. She claimed she was using a translation app, but she didn't have her phone near her." The name Donati filled Kate's brain. Why hadn't she tried her grandparents' names? Could Donati be Alessa and Piero's last name? Her mom's maiden name?

"Great. Hiding something again."

Kate bit her lip as the photographs of the dead people shuffled through her mind once more.

"How could your mom be Italian? She doesn't have the skin of an Italian. She's white as a ghost and has blue eyes." Ellie tapped her fingers on the desk.

"Yes. You know how she stays out of the sun, but despite that, people think we look alike. They think she is my birth mother. There is something Italian in her look. Something that connects us."

"Well, I hate to break this to you, but your birth mother and father are alive and therefore would not be on a pedigree chart. You don't know your birth grandparents' names do you?"

"No. I know. I don't know what I'm doing." Kate put her hands on the sides of her head, leaned her elbows on the desk, and huffed. She should have looked for Donatis.

"I'll tell you what you are doing, you are stalling. You're afraid to find the very information you crave." Ellie put her arm around Kate. "You can do this. It'll be okay."

Kate nodded, pressing her lips together into a frown. Ellie's hug felt nice. She forced her fingers to type Carmela's name. Tons of records popped up. "There are thousands of records. We don't have time to go through them all."

"Put in Venice. You think she's from here, right?"

"Maybe, but we don't know for sure."

Kate put in "Venice." She stared at the screen. "Ten." She scrolled through the documents and could see her birth mother's name on each one, but nothing that looked like it could belong to her.

She put in Vincenzo Bellini—nothing, just like she expected. Both girls stared at the screen. "We can't find her if we don't know her maiden name."

"Or, if she's alive or simply not in there."

"You could find her christening or baptism or marriage."

"If it's in there."

The librarian came back. "Find anything? Need me to translate?" She looked excited, happy to help. Her bright red lipstick flashed as she talked.

"Sure. What are these?" Kate pulled up the screen with ten Carmela Bellinis listed and then clicked on one of the records.

"This one is a state record of a death for Carmela Bellini." She went down the information on the side. "Death date: 1850, death place: Napoli, Italy, gender: female, Age: 27, Birth place: Napoli, and year: 1823. Is this who you were looking for?"

"No. Too old."

"Let me see if we can narrow the search. If we consider your age and the possible ages of your parents, we can get a range of dates. I'd say about 80 years from today probably."

"My parents aren't 80." Kate laughed despite herself.

"I hope not, I just like to go wide when it comes to this program." Kate put in that date range along with her birth mother's name but there were no results. "It looks like you are out of luck with this database. Were they Catholic by chance?"

"I believe so." Really, Kate knew so.

"If your parents were born here, you can go directly to the church to look at the records. There are a lot of Catholic churches in Venice that haven't had their records indexed or allowed into Family Search." She shook her phone as if that told them everything. "But, since you know she's a Bellini, we can narrow down which churches you should go to, to check the records."

Kate's stomach churned. "They let you look at the records?"

"Of course. And, you wouldn't need to look back very far, so it shouldn't take very long. Since she is a Bellini, I suggest Basilica di Santa Maria della Salute. It's kind of out of the way, but definitely the hot spot for the Bellinis."

"What do you mean, the hot spot for the Bellinis?"

"Oh, sorry, I forget that you aren't from here. There are thousands of Bellinis here and they all like to go to the same couple of churches. If the records aren't at Santa Maria you should check out Saint Mark's Basilica.

"Feel free to explore as much as you like with this program. Oh, and if you're looking for your grandmother, it's best to have a maiden name." She smiled with those red lips and left again.

"Venice is a hotbed for Bellinis?" Kate said.

Ellie visibly shuddered and then scanned the room.

Kate stared at the screen and noticed she had keyed in Carmela without the L. Her heart pounded and she set her hands above the keys to type the name correctly when she felt a heavy hand on her shoulder. She twisted, catching sight of Ellie's eyes as she did. They were focused on someone standing behind her. It made Kate turn even faster, her heart a racing train.

Duran's soft brown eyes met hers as he stepped back three steps, his hand brushing through his shaggy mane.

15

"Duran?" Kate almost stood up to hug him, but his posture and the serious look on his face made her stay seated. She drew in a deep breath. A quiver of anticipation rushed through her. Duran was only feet from her. She wanted to run her hands through his longish dark hair.

"What are you doing here, Kate?" A big dip appeared between his eyes. There was something off about him, not right. It made her feel defensive.

"I could ask you the same thing." She fought to conquer her nerves. This wasn't how seeing Duran again should have gone.

"I needed some space from the family and this is one of the only places they don't follow me. But you?" He shook his head and ran a hand over his mouth and chin.

"No. I meant, what are you doing in Italy." She gripped the chair to help her stay seated.

"It's a long story and I don't have a lot of time." He shifted from foot to foot, obviously impatient.

"I think you'd better tell me that story."

He sighed. "No. All you need to know is that you have to get the heck out of here." His eyes scanned the room and beyond, past the windows.

"What are you talking about?"

"Venice. It's full of Bellinis and not just any Bellinis, but Bellinis from New Jersey. Bellinis who know who you are."

"What are you talking about?"

He sighed again. "I guess I'm not going to get out of telling you." He pointed at Ellie. "Help me shut the blinds, Ellie."

"Just spit it out." Kate was having a hard time wrapping her brain around the fact that Duran was here and she wasn't in his arms and there didn't appear to be any chance of that changing.

Neither Ellie nor Kate moved. Duran maneuvered the cords on the blinds until the windows were covered, muttering to himself the whole time. No one from outside the room would be able to see what was happening inside. Then he glanced quickly over at Kate who was staring intently at him, before saying, "Look. After the raid at the Marconi club, they sent everyone who was brought to FBI headquarters to Italy. Well, almost everyone."

He was standing too far from her. She wanted to move to him. "But you weren't there, at the raid." Kate's mind raced through her mental list of who was at the club and who was at the airport.

"No, but they sent me anyway. Most of the people being sent away were Marconis, and they wanted to ship out some Bellinis and others so it didn't look as obvious. They sent us all at different times, too. The last ones got here only a week ago I understand."

In the back of her mind the fact that Duran had saved her gave her hope. He had been her salvation.

"But seriously. You've got to get out of here. You should catch the next plane out. A good 75% of the people in that raid at Marconi's club are in Italy right now."

"Is Vinny here then?" She wanted to reach out and touch him. She wished she could tell him Vinny was her dad.

"No. They wanted to send him, but Salvatorio got sick and since Vinny is number two, he had to stay." Duran shoved his hands into his pockets.

"What do you mean, number two?"

"He's the oldest son. If anything happens to his dad, he's supposed to take over."

"But?"

"But the other brothers are more motivated. Who knows what will happen there." He kept glancing around the small room.

"You think they might try to kill him?"

"I don't know, but it seems like a good possibility." He moved to a window and looked out behind the blinds.

"It must be hard here, not speaking Italian." She wasn't sure why she said it. There were so many other things she wanted to say. He was so close and all she wanted to do was grab him up in her arms, but his stance, his words, all told her to stay back.

"I already speak Italian."

"You hid that from me?" Her head jerked back slightly in shock.

"It just never came up. They'd have their meetings and I couldn't understand a thing. I learned it out of self-defense, so I'd know what they were saying."

Something about that sent heat to her chest. "Oh, Duran. I could so use your translating skills. I can't read these documents."

"Oh, no. I can't. I need to leave. I've been here too long." He glanced again at the covered windows.

She couldn't stand it one more second. "I can't believe it's you." She stood up and moved toward him, leaving Ellie sitting, gawking at the two of them.

"Stop." He held his hands out.

Kate flinched.

"We got sidetracked," Duran said. "The only thing that matters is that we get you out of Venice. Now." He shook his head and actually looked mad or possibly disappointed. "After everything, you show up here? How?"

She didn't want to talk about that. She had things she wanted and needed to say. "I know what you did." Kate took another step toward him. "It took everything I had not to send you a letter, a text, an email to thank you for saving me. Thank you and I'm sorry for not treating you how I should have while I was there." She reached up for his cheek, but he jerked away.

"No. Don't do this. Please." His words gradually got quieter and almost sounded like a prayer.

She didn't let him stop her. With her hand still outstretched, she reached him, placing her palm on his cheek. Yet again he jerked away. "I can't believe it's you."

A strangled cry came out of his mouth from somewhere deep down. "I never thought I'd see you again. What are you doing here?"

"I'm here to find my parents."

"What? I thought that was why you were in Jersey."

"It was. My birth mother is here, though." She knew she couldn't tell him the whole truth and most definitely couldn't tell him about Vinny, and it was killing her. He looked so pained already.

"You're kidding, right?"

"No. She's from Venice and I have to find her."

"You already know she's here?" His hands dropped to his sides.

"Yes."

"Then go home. Leave here. Come back in a few years after everything's been settled and no one remembers you."

Kate shook her head. "I can't do that."

"Please, Kate. Please. It's too hot for you to be here right now. If someone spotted you, it would not be good."

"I'm sorry. I have to find her. I have to."

"Why? Why do you insist on putting yourself in danger? It was bad enough when you showed back up at the bagel shop in Jersey, thinking you could somehow save me. I could have gotten out of it on my own. I only needed to wait it out."

"Not if they beat you to death." Saying it out loud caused her heart to ache a little, and she realized she would do anything for this guy. She touched his face again but he jerked away, again.

"I can't. I said goodbye to you already." The sadness in his eyes caused hers to burn and her chin to tremble.

"But a hello is much better." Her chest ached.

He grimaced.

"I promise as soon as I find her, I'll leave. I'm sure it will be today." Her lips parted slightly and she stared hard at him.

"No." The word came out like a muted cry. "Go now. They will kill you and it won't be an easy death. They will torture you and hurt you until you wish you were dead and just when you are barely hanging on to life, that's when they will kill you." His voice rose in pitch and almost turned to a whine.

"It's only for one day. I'm not going to let them catch me." It had to be true.

He put his hands on her arms and she closed her eyes. His touch was all she needed. "You've got to go. Please. If you ever cared for me, you will go."

She stomped one foot and he let go of her. "You know I care about you. That's the hard part. I wish I could go. This is something I have to do and it doesn't reflect on how I feel about you. I promise to leave right after I find her."

"You are so stubborn." He spoke through gritted teeth. His breathing was hard and his eyes turned cold.

"It's not like they are going to know. Like you said, everything is in upheaval, and they won't notice me."

Like a lightning bolt of realization hit him, his face changed, becoming resolute and serious. "Don't draw attention to yourself. Use a different name. Blend in." He was backing away toward the door. He was leaving?

"You know who I'm with, right? Two people who don't blend in." They both looked at Ellie, who didn't look at all ashamed at her eavesdropping. Had Colby been there, he would have received the look too.

"Get glasses. Big glasses. The eyes are what give most people away.

Get a scarf. Put something over your hair. Try to walk differently. Talk quietly. That means you too, Ellie." His voice was shaking by the time he got to the end. "This is not good."

Kate needed to change the subject. She needed to make him stay somehow. "So, Bellini Bagels is here?" She inched forward.

"No. I'm at Francessco's Restaurant. The families don't want a clear and definite connection to them in the States. They like to keep things separate. I even have to use a nickname while I'm here."

"A nickname, huh? What is it?"

"Ran."

"Interesting. The last half of your name?"

He nodded. "I'm sorry your trip had to be interrupted, but you truly are in danger here. You have to go as quickly as possible."

"Don't worry. Tonight we head back to Bologna," she said in a quiet voice. Now that she'd seen him, she didn't want to leave him.

"Bologna? Let me guess, you flew into the Marconi airport."

Kate nodded and heat rushed up her neck. She was dimly aware that Ellie cleared her throat, but Kate didn't look her way. "Yeah. Ellie's brother is at the University of Bologna."

Duran's eyebrows scrunched together and his eyes narrowed. "No. Oh, no. That is Marconi headquarters. All the Marconis who were sent back are there."

"Seriously?"

"Seriously. I'm heading there in a few weeks to finish my schooling. Then I'll become an earner and you know what comes next."

"No. You can't become an associate."

"I don't really have a choice. My path is laid out before me. I follow it or I die."

"Come with us tonight. We can catch a plane together. You could live with me and leave this life."

"I can't do that. I would lead them right to you. They don't trust me, remember? Their people are all over that place. I would be seen and you'd be compromised. It's the Marconi freaking airport. Who do you

135

think runs and owns it?" He grunted. "Argh! I can't believe you are here."

"I can't believe you're here either." She had to say what she was thinking or she'd explode. "All I want to do is hold you in my arms, but you're not making it easy."

"Well," he said, looking away. "You have everything you need. I'll be going now."

"No."

"And when and if you find your family, don't let them persuade you to stay. They will try, Kate. Family is everything to Italians."

She was reminded of how Colby and Martino had said the same thing and wondered if it was one of the rules about being Italian that Martino would have taught her. Her cheeks flamed.

"They'll want to keep you. I hope they are good people. I hope your birth mother embraces you. And remember, not everything is as it appears. Italians can be cruel, selfish, not caring about anything but themselves, and so power hungry, even when it's only the person receiving the power who knows of it."

Kate couldn't help but think that the same could be said about Americans. Then in a heated rush, Duran stepped away from the door and grabbed her, kissing her passionately on the lips. Deep tingles fired throughout her body and seemed to collect in her heart, creating a massive surge of adrenaline. He tried to pull away, but she held him in a hug for several seconds before releasing him. When he looked at her, his eyes glistened and he whispered. "No more secrets, Kate."

She wanted to whisper the same words back, but she knew that sometimes secrets had to be kept. Before he left, he looked at her like he knew she was holding something back.

Kate's insides roiled. Why had she let him go? She turned to Ellie, who was crying. "That was the most beautiful and sad thing I've ever seen. Katiebug, we've got to listen to him and get the heck out of here."

"I can't leave. I can't. I'm too close." She moved to Ellie.

Ellie stood. "We are getting out of here. You and me. You said you didn't want to put me in danger."

"I don't. What happened to, *I'll go into danger for you*?"

Sorrow filled Ellie's eyes and she looked ashamed.

"It's okay. I want you to leave. I want you to go back. Go back to Bologna without me. You're not in danger except when you're with me. So go. I seriously want you to go."

"No. You're coming with me." Ellie balled up her little fists.

"I can't do that." Kate stood firm. She knew there was no way Ellie would be able to force her to return.

"You are so stubborn, Kate Hamilton. Did you not hear what he said? Feel what he said? Even I felt that. I've never felt anything like that... Come on. Come with me." She took a step toward Kate and took one of her hands.

"No." Kate shook her head. "No. You go. I mean it. Go." She squeezed Ellie's hand and then let go of it.

"I'm calling Colby." Ellie dug out her phone and punched in his number.

"Fine. But, you are going and I am staying. You should fly home, but if you are going to Bologna, to your brother, then lie low."

"Don't be ridiculous." She put her phone up to her ear. "You are coming with me."

"No. I'm not. Accept it."

"Colby!" Ellie almost screamed into the phone.

Kate turned to the computer, added the missing L to Carmela's name and clicked on the button, sending her birth mother's correctly spelled name into the search engine of the database. In the background she could hear Ellie talking to Colby.

One name popped up.

Birth date forty years previous and death date fifteen.

16

Kate could no longer hear Ellie's voice. In fact, a loud humming seemed to fill her whole soul. As if on autopilot, she selected the name. A death certificate popped up on the screen. Carmela Bellini. Born in Venice, Italy. Died in New Jersey, United States of America. Several pictures of her and one of her grave were available. The location of the grave: Venice, Italy. Despite feeling like stone, Kate's fingers still seemed to have enough flexibility to click on the link. Three pictures of her birth mother popped up. One as a baby, one as a teen, and one as an adult. It was definitely her. There was no question. And the headstone left no doubt. Her mother was dead, her body interred at the Venice cemetery. Kate drew in a quick breath.

She was barely aware of Ellie hugging her. She must have seen what Kate had discovered. Ellie was still talking on the phone. "No. Never mind. We'll be back tonight and fly out tomorrow.

"I'm so sorry, Kate. I'm so, so sorry." Ellie squeezed Kate, but Kate remained unaware. After a while Ellie clicked some buttons on the computer and Kate heard the printer spring to life. Ellie also took some pictures of the computer screen. Kate was still, staring.

"I don't mean to rush you, Kate, but the next train leaves in twenty minutes. It's like someone is watching out for you. Like Carmela made sure you found this information so you could feel okay about leaving and be safe. It's like perfect and terrible timing all at once. Now we can go back to Bologna together. There's no one to see. I'm very, very sorry, but we have to go."

"No." Kate's words came out as a whisper as she stared flatly at the screen.

"What? What did you say?" Ellie walked over and grabbed the papers from the printer.

"No. I've got to go to the grave. You go. Go to the train station. I know I'm putting myself in danger, but I have to go see the grave."

"You're being reckless right now because you're hurting. I'm not going to let you stay. I know I'm the one who encouraged you to come here and find your birth mother, but Duran is right. We should leave."

"I am going to the grave. I'm sorry Ellie. I'm here now, and we'll never be back. It has to be now." Every muscle in Kate's body tensed as she pushed her shoulders back and stood. Nothing was going to get in the way of her seeing that grave.

"No. I'll make sure we come back in a few years like Duran suggested. We'll make sure it's safe and we'll come and visit the grave together. We'll stay all day if you want. I swear. I'll make it happen." She gave Kate a pained stare and rubbed her upper arms, obviously needing some comfort herself.

"No. Go, Ellie. Go now." Kate pushed on her, but gently.

"Kate, please." Ellie was blubbering now, scared. Kate stood and hugged her tight.

"I'll be okay. I need to do this, and I need to know you are safe while I do."

Ellie huffed, "No!"

This was not a good time for Ellie to become stubborn. Kate would have to make her go. She didn't want to hurt her friend, but Kate couldn't have Ellie stay and be in danger any longer.

Kate's eyes pierced Ellie's. "I don't expect you to come with me. In fact, I don't want you to come with me. This is your fault. You're the one who pushed me to go looking for my mother and we found her. She's dead. In the ground. All alone. I have to tell her I'm okay. I have to. But you go. You go back home to your perfect life. Your perfect *living* family. Go, Ellie. Go now!"

Ellie was crying. "Stop it, Kate. You're just upset."

"No. I want you to go." She pushed on Ellie until she was out the door. "Go!"

Ellie's face had contorted into something like anger. She stomped her foot and said, "No."

Kate closed her eyes and breathed deeply. She'd never get rid of Ellie like this. She needed a better plan. With a huff, she said, "Fine. Let's go."

"I know it's hard, but you are too important to me, Kate. I would never leave you here alone, not with the Bellinis all over the place. Not with you being in so much danger. This is the right decision. We'll come back, I promise."

Kate dropped her head and said, "You have the information about the grave? Pictures?"

"Yes." She waved the printed pages. "I took pictures of all the screens about Carmela and printed off what I could."

"Could you send me the pictures?" Kate took the printed pages and put them in her backpack.

"Of course."

"Now?"

"I will when we get to the train station. We are going to have to run."

Kate nodded. "Let's go, then." She still didn't feel like she had control of her own body. It was like it was on autopilot.

Ellie gave her a quick relieved smile before leading the way out of the library. Once outside, she said, "We should keep our heads down."

Kate nodded and they jogged, heads down, all the way to the terminal. They went straight for a machine to buy their tickets. With two minutes to spare and completely out of breath, they climbed onto the train.

Ellie took a seat next to the window and Kate put her hand on the back of her seat. "I'm not feeling so great. I'm headed to the Loo."

"Want me to go with you?" People were filing onto the train, bustling past them and taking their seats.

"No. I don't want to lose our seats. I'll be right back. Send me those pics."

"Okay." Ellie pulled out a water bottle from her purse and grabbed her phone.

Kate took one long look at the back of Ellie's head and then walked toward the back of the train, but instead of going all the way to the toilet, she took the steps that led out of the train and onto the platform. Ellie would be so mad, but this was the only way. She wouldn't even know Kate was missing until the train was already on its way back to Bologna.

Without looking back, Kate headed to library and walked to the Harry Potter study hall to find the librarian who had helped her earlier. "Could you tell me how I get to this cemetery?" She held out the paper with the name on it.

The librarian led her out of the room. "So, you found what you needed? I'm so glad." Her smile was warm. "I can't tell you how nice it was to help you today. Usually, I'm working with old, dusty texts and it's nice to work on more current things. Walk down to the main drag there, where all the ships are docking and take the vaporetto, uh, water boat 4.1 or 4.2. It's only a five minute ride to the island."

"It's on an island?"

"Yes. It used to be a prison and now there's a church and the cemetery. It's quite peaceful."

"Thank you. Vaporetto 4.1 or 4.2."

"Yes."

Kate wished she could cry. Instead she went straight to the boat dock, stopping only long enough to buy a huge vase with bright flowers from a street vendor. After paying the fare, she boarded the vaporetto for Isola di San Michele, an entire island for the dead. The boat was almost full, the water was calm, and the ride smooth. She could see everyone talking all around her, but couldn't hear any one conversation. Her mind was fixed on her birth mother and the island that came toward her. Her mother was gone. Really gone. She wasn't an FBI agent. They couldn't find her because she was in a grave in Italy.

Because she was the last one on, Kate was the first to get off the boat. Although the church at the corner of the island was wonderfully cool and austere, Kate could not appreciate the sad beauty of it. And while the cemetery itself was wide and calm, a series of huge gardens studded with cypress trees and awful monuments, Kate's heart rushed and thudded.

The whole area was cluttered with hundreds of thousands of tombs—some lavishly monumental, with domes and sculptures and wrought-iron gates, some stacked in high modern terraces, like filing systems. She grabbed a plot map, oriented herself and followed the paths that appeared to lead her to Carmela's grave. As she walked she passed row after row of pure-white blocks of columbarium, colorfully decorated with flowers and pictures of the deceased. Rows of small white crosses filled the next area and then large tombstones. What struck her right off was the quiet that pervaded the island. An island to cradle the dead on the sea.

Finally, she came upon the grave. It was simple, a white cross that was aging in spots to a dull gray. The name, Carmela Bellini was unmistakable. Kate fell to her knees, setting the flowers near the headstone, and wailed, beating at the small patch of ground surrounding the stone. The tears that had built up in her exploded. Her mother was really dead. The proof was before her eyes. She would never see, touch, or smell her mother again. It was not fair. Not right.

Finally, when no more tears would come, she leaned up against the cross and talked to her mother, telling her all about her life. About that time in fifth grade when she ran into the glass wall, about her first boyfriend, and Duran. About her adoptive parents and siblings and how much she loved them. How lucky she felt to have such a great family.

After a time, she noticed a second cross next to Carmela's with Vincenzo's name on it. It had his birth date, but no death date. She stood and noticed this was a family plot and there, on the other side of her birth mother's grave was another. The cross had her name on it. Her Italian name: Constanzie Bellini. Kate whipped around and then knelt down, staring at the cross with her name. Her pre-adoption name. She'd supposedly died only days after her mother. Wait. She glanced back at her mother's grave. Then she stood and said, "I am not dead," to the quiet, peaceful island. An offering of truth.

She, Kate, wasn't dead. What if Carmela really wasn't dead either?

Just as she chastised herself for thinking it, her memories burst open.

Kate sat on a piano bench in a large hall. Carmela finished playing a beautiful piece and then smiled down at her daughter's three-year-old frame. The room erupted with applause. Her birth mother was so beautiful. Flawless in a navy blue couture gown and hair lifted off her neck in a fancy supermodel style.

"It's your turn now, honey," she said as she moved slightly to the side.

Little Kate slid to the middle of the bench and put her hands to the keys. She played and played, and the audience clapped and clapped when she finished. Then she stood with her mother and the auditorium rocked with applause. They wanted an encore. Carmela nodded at her to begin playing again. The audience fell silent. Kate began to play, looking up at her birth mother and her birth mother looking down at her, her smile radiant. A boom sounded in the hall and Kate covered her ears as Carmela flopped forward, her head falling to the keys with a clang. Little Kate felt something warm on her cheek and turned toward the screaming crowds. She tapped her birth mother's leg. "Mommy. Mommy!" Then she was rushed away in someone's arms as people attended to her mom.

Seventeen-year-old Kate grabbed at her hair and screamed. The memory that had been locked deep inside her was now completely in the open.

She sat, staring at nothing, but aware of the sun moving across the sky. It was time to go. There was nothing more for her here. She knew without her father having to tell her now that the hit had been ordered by the Marconis and the Bellinis had allowed it. Her grandfather Salvatorio had allowed the Marconis to kill her mother, otherwise, the shot would never have happened. No wonder her father wouldn't tell her what had happened.

Somehow, she needed to make them pay.

She was only one person. An insignificant person at that. She had no skills. It was only wishful and desperate thinking that she could do anything to hurt them like they'd hurt her.

Kate stood and brushed off her pants and ran her fingers through her hair. As she did this, she noticed the area next to her family's plot had six graves, what looked like the children, parents, and grandparents. Her gaze swept her family's plot. There seemed to be space for others. But who? Her grandparents? Were they still alive? Her birth mother was born here, maybe her parents, Kate's grandparents, still lived here. As if the Heavens had opened an idea rang inside her head.

She could find her grandparents and tell them who she was. Show them she was still alive and not dead. That could be her revenge. It was a small act of defiance, but something nonetheless. She knew exactly how to find out if they were alive. She scampered back to the dock and got on the first vaporetto that showed up. The numbness had gone and a direct focus filled her. It was like her brain started working at last and she could feel the hot sun on her skin again. As she scanned the faces on the boat, they all looked familiar and seemed to be looking at her. Her leg muscles tightened, but she had nowhere to run. Instead, she pressed her elbows into her sides, trying to make herself as small as possible, trying to disappear. She stared at her feet, holding back a scream. She knew she was being paranoid, but she couldn't seem to help it. The Bellinis would not take her. Not yet. She had to get to her grandparents before the Bellinis got to her.

The five minutes it took to get back to the main island seemed to take hours and her stomach felt rock hard by the time she stepped off the boat. She rushed away, glancing back to see if anyone was following her. Once she decided she wasn't being followed, she stopped at the first shop she came to and bought a light scarf that she wrapped around her head, hiding her hair. Then she grabbed some large sunglasses and finally a jacket before heading to the library where she pulled up Family Search and located Carmela's records again. There were no links to Carmela's parents. A good sign. No pedigree chart linking them meant they could possibly be alive.

There was only one problem. She didn't know their names.

She couldn't find them without names. She didn't even know Carmela's maiden name. She clicked back to Carmela's death record and was surprised to see that no parents' names were listed. Kate sat staring at the computer for several moments until she remembered what the librarian had said about finding things in church documents. The marriage record was sure to have her grandparents' names on it. It had to.

Kate didn't want to go to the church that was full of Bellinis and expose herself to the clergy. She knew from her experience in New Jersey that if the Bellinis frequented that church, the priest was most likely neck deep in the family business. She'd have to be very careful not to call too much attention to herself. She thought about it and it occurred to her what she could do and it just might work. But she'd have to make a few stops on the way for supplies.

17

Kate made her way to the church after strengthening her disguise and hiding the locket beneath her clothes. As the librarian had said, the church was off the beaten path, quiet and empty. The other churches near the main square bustled with tourists, lines flowing out the doors. She walked to the front and a priest came out. He was tall and thin with a pinched face. "*Buon pomeriggio.*"

"Do you happen to speak English?" she said, trying to act naturally, but she couldn't help but push on the prescription-less glasses she'd found to help with her disguise indoors. It wasn't like she could wear sunglasses into the church.

"I do." His thinning hair was slicked back and looked wet. He pressed his lips together.

"Great. I was wondering if I could look at the wedding records from these years for a project I'm working on." She held out the sheet of paper.

"That's a lot of records. Maybe if you could tell me specifically what you are looking for I might be able to direct you." He tapped his index finger on one of the pews.

"Actually, that's the fun of this project. I'm not exactly sure what I'm looking for. Just anything that catches my eye that I want to run with.”

"Okay. You can come back here to the records room. But know that these are precious documents with important information. They are not to be played with." He swayed more than walked back to the room.

"The records for those years are here." He swung his arm out with a flourish, indicating a room to his left. "Please use these gloves and no flash photography." He picked up some gloves from a shelf outside the door of the room and handed them to her. "I'll be just outside if you need anything. And no food or drink. Not even gum." He rounded his lips to pop the m-sound on gum.

"Thank you so much." She smiled as she stepped toward the room.

He gave her a curt nod as a bulky man came barreling down the hallway. Kate held her breath and looked around for anything that could possibly be used as a weapon. Nothing, only books. She was trapped. But, the big man didn't seem to pay much attention to her. He gave her a hasty glance and led the priest farther down the hall. A note of recognition flared at the back of her mind. She had seen that man before, but where? She shook her head. She was being paranoid. Every person she saw seemed familiar now. She stared into the room with volumes and volumes of books, then entered. She would be quick. Pulling down the first volume she flipped through the pages, stopping on a few entries and taking a picture then jotting down some random notes. She repeated the same actions with each volume just in case she was being watched. Because she had Carmela's birthdate from the tombstone she had a better idea what years to search through. When she got to the one she really wanted, she flipped through it more slowly than the others until she found what she needed: the marriage record. Both of her grandparents' names were there. She snapped the picture and jotted down some notes then continued to the next volume, doing the same with a few more records selected at random. She forced herself to stay a little longer taking some additional miscellaneous pictures. When she was done, she put the books back on the shelf and made her way toward the exit.

The man who had run into her before she went into the records room stepped out in front of her, crossing his arms over his large chest. At that moment, it occurred to her how she knew him. Her heartbeat crashed in her ears, and she clenched her jaw as she pushed up against the doorjamb. He was the man Benito and Galtem had gone to the airport to pick up when they'd run into her trying to escape. Ricco. He'd only glanced at her at best.

"Do I know you?" he asked in English that was barely understandable behind the strong Italian accent.

He had recognized her after all. She had to get him off her trail. "Not unless you're from Tennessee. You from there?" she asked, laying on a thick accent of her own. "I've only been two places in my life: Tennessee and Italy."

He narrowed his eyes and said, "Tennessee?"

She nodded.

"You look so familiar, that's all."

"Guess you've seen my twin then." She smiled and a warning filled her gut, telling her to get out of there. She realized by saying that, she was making him search his memory even more. "Well, I've got to get going. Have a nice day, now." As soon as she turned the corner, she whipped out her sunglasses and raced to the first store she could find that sold scarves and jackets. She bought another jacket and two more scarves. If something happened to give her away again, she wanted to be prepared.

She opened the door to leave and noticed Ricco across the street, talking to someone. His head whipped around at the sound of the little bell tinkling on the door as she opened it. His eyes lit on her and she was about to run when she remembered she had all new clothes and glasses on. She tried to act natural, and realizing she had stopped in the doorway, forced her feet to take her out onto the path. Ricco's gaze lingered on her for a few seconds, then he turned back to the person he'd been talking to. Kate exhaled sharply and walked, swinging the bag from the shop that held all her old clothes and a few new ones. Her brain buzzed with fear, afraid he'd somehow known it was her and followed her. Her desire to turn and look was strong, but she fought against it. She would only check if he was behind her when she entered the library because it would be natural for her to look behind her as she swung the door open. The farther she got from the church without being accosted, the less stressed she felt. Certainly if he had been following her, he would have approached her by then.

Realizing she was still far from the library and that it was probably going to close soon, she stopped at an Internet café and used a site Ellie had showed her to search for her grandparents.

To her surprise, there was only one search result. Kate put the address into her phone and executed another search. It would take her half an hour to get to their home according to her maps app, but maybe she would finally get to meet her birth grandparents. She left the Internet café and started on her path. She hadn't walked far before she felt someone following her. She glanced around, but saw no one. Could it be Ricco? No. She was being paranoid. He hadn't followed her to the Internet café. Shaking it off, she kept going. Another block down, the feeling returned. She glanced around again. The feeling of being watched was unmistakable. She picked up the pace and went into the first shop she came upon. She pretended to shop and kept looking out the window, but saw no one. She decided to go again, but left out a back door when the shopkeeper was helping another customer. Unless she picked up the pace, she'd never make it to her grandparents'.

Kate hurried as she walked and thanked God that it was still light outside as she followed the complicated directions on her phone. She decided to do as she'd learned in her self-defense classes. She would stand straight, walk purposefully, and fake a confidence she didn't feel. The feeling of being followed hadn't returned. She had given whoever was following her the slip, or maybe there was no one in the first place. Twenty-two minutes later, she'd reached her destination. Kate stood staring at a home sandwiched between two others when all her insecurities reached out and grabbed her. She wanted her grandparents to want her. She took in a deep breath and climbed the ten steps. She took another deep breath and rang the doorbell.

An older gentleman came to the door. "*Excusi*," Kate said. Then she read the names from the marriage license. She was sure she'd butchered them, and felt ridiculous that she hadn't asked someone to pronounce them for her.

The man did not respond, but stared at her instead, a confused or possibly fearful look on his face. "You don't speak English do you?"

He shook his head, but continued to stare. A woman came to the door and Kate repeated the names. She hadn't considered the possibility that neither would speak English and they wouldn't be able to communicate. The man said something to the woman and she narrowed her eyes, her head leaning slightly to the right. Kate sighed and said to the air, "What do I do now?" She looked up at the sky, her hand going to her locket as it always did when she worried. When she let her head fall forward, the woman pushed on the door, staring at Kate's chest. Instinctively, Kate took a step back.

"*No. No. Excusi.*" The screen door was open now and the woman held her hands out, palms up as she motioned to Kate's neck. Kate looked down and saw the locket. The locket! They'd recognized the locket. She unclasped it and held it out to them. The woman opened it and started to cry, opening her arms to Kate, ushering her into the house.

The woman talked and talked, all in Italian, and even though Kate thought they understood who she was and how desperately she wanted to get to know them, her inability to communicate with them fully was giving her a headache. Kate finally pointed to herself and said, "Constanzie". Both of them nodded and hugged Kate. They kissed her cheeks and her hands and then guided her to the back of the house towared a small, grassy, flower filled backyard with a nice fountain. Kate saw someone in a wheelchair near the fountain. Her grandmother went down the steps and the man, her grandfather, encouraged her, with a nod of his head to follow. She walked down a wooden ramp next to the stairs.

Her grandmother took her hand and led her straight to the person in the chair, whose back was to them, facing the fountain. She had long brown hair, and the few strands that sat in a patch of late afternoon sunshine shone in the light. Kate felt a bit curious about this person she was about to meet.

They rounded the chair and Kate's world stopped. Her hand left the comfort of her grandma's and flew to her mouth as a gasp left it.

Kate stared at the unseeing eyes before her. She took the last step forward and fell to her knees, her head resting on the woman's lap for a few seconds before she clasped her hands in hers and kissed them, just as her grandmother had done only moments before. The woman gave no reaction, only sat there, staring past them.

Carmela, her mother, was alive!

Kate's tears wet her mother's hands until she could compose herself. Her grandpa was now standing with his arm around her grandma, their happy gazes looking down at the scene before them.

Kate sniffed and rubbed her nose on her sleeve. She rose and pressed her lips to her mother's forehead before resting her forehead on her mom's. Her mom smelled like roses and some unfamiliar spice. "Mom. I love you. I can't believe it's you. I can't believe you're alive."

Kate needed answers and she wouldn't get them this way. She needed an interpreter, and she knew just where to find one. He wouldn't want to do it, but he was the only person she knew in Venice she could trust. She stood.

"I need to go." She used her hands to try to explain to her grandparents what was about to happen. "I will be back. I'll bring someone to interpret."

They shook their heads like they thought Kate was going to do something bad. Her grandma put her finger to her lips and made the *shhh* sound. Her grandpa was saying something in Italian, frenzied and worried. Kate went to her grandma and nodded. "*Sì*. I won't tell anyone she's here. It's a secret. I get it. *Shhh!*" Kate repeated. "*Shhh!*"

They smiled. "I'm going but I will be back tonight. I won't tell anyone. She is safe." Kate hugged Carmela, then her granparents as well.

She ran through the house, grabbed her bag from the sofa, but left her shopping bag next to the couch and hurried out the front door, a rush of hope enveloping her as she raced through the narrow streets of Venice, forgetting that she needed to hide until she saw her pursuer as she turned a corner. His eyes met her uncovered ones and they both seemed to freeze. Comprehension must have dawned on Ricco, because his strong legs propelled him toward her. She stepped back around the corner, her legs unwilling to cooperate. She ran, but knew she was at a disadvantage. She didn't know the streets like he did. She would be captured. She should have listened to Duran and Ellie. Before Kate could round the corner to the other side of the building, he grabbed her bag and dragged her to the ground, pinning her with his knee on her chest and his hands pressing hers into the ground, her knuckles scraping on the cobbled path.

"You are that girl from the airport. The girl that sent Galtem to prison. Salvatorio shouldn't have sent you here. He always was overconfident." He sneered.

She could barely breathe, air coming in shallow bursts. She tried to move her hands, but he was too strong and he shifted, his other leg lying across hers. It occurred to Kate that Ricco wasn't where he should be. He was a Marconi and not supposed be in Venice. He should be in Bologna. His encounter with the priest now took on new meaning. It had been an unfriendly meeting for sure. The only thing she had going for her was that he apparently didn't know she was AWOL from the Bellini family. Not that it mattered, because Ricco wouldn't be taking her to Bellinis, he'd be taking her to Marconis. It wasn't an improvement.

"*Eh!*" Someone shouted and footsteps pounded toward them. One of Ricco's hands flew to his jacket pocket and pulled out a gun. That was all Kate needed. Her free hand whipped up to his face and scratched at his eyes. His other hand left hers and swiped wildly at her clawing hands. The man who screamed had reached them and knocked the gun from

Ricco's hand. A shot fired into the building next to them. More feet stomped their way. Who were these people coming to help her? If any were Bellinis she would not fare well.

Ricco rolled off her, pushing the man who had come to save her to the ground. Kate tried to catch her breath as she rolled to her knees and stood up. She grabbed her purse from the ground and pushed through the small crowd of people who'd assembled. Several women tried to stop her, grabbing at her with pained expressions of sympathy and saying words that Kate could only guess were pleas to help her. She brushed them off and kept going, running blindly down the path until she found a café to slip into, and heading straight for the bathroom to splash water onto her face. She should leave, catch the next train out of there and fly home. A sob built just thinking about the reality of the situation. Her birth mother was alive, but living a life no one should have to. Because of the Marconis and Bellinis.

Kate didn't want to wait too long in case Ricco escaped the mob of people that had descended on him and started looking for her again.

She turned her jacket inside out, pulled her hair up and put on some big glasses. She forced herself to walk casually, hoping to look like she belonged. Once she reached St. Mark's Square, she kept to the crowds, her head down. Her stomach growled as she passed several restaurants until she saw a sign that read, Francessco's. Duran's restaurant. She couldn't help herself. She stopped and looked around, browsing the tables that sat in the square. No sight of Duran. Her eyes whipped to the building and she caught a glimpse of him taking an order from a guest. As if he felt her looking, his head snapped up, their eyes meeting. She wanted to go inside and talk to him, but knew she couldn't. She commanded her legs to move and her head to look away. The tears filling her eyes were making it hard for her to see. She swiped at them as she rushed past several shops, getting closer and closer to her goal.

She rushed down the stairs of the railway station and headed for the ticket kiosk. But as she passed the restrooms, she was shoved inside. She tried to scream, but a hand covered her mouth. She opened her mouth and tried to bite the hand, but a voice stopped her. "Kate. It's me, Duran."

She froze, then melted into him, sobbing.

He reached over and locked the door, cradling her in his arms. "Shhh! It's okay. Where's Ellie?"

"Bologna. I think. I sent her away."

"You're here alone?"

She nodded and looked up at him, wiping her nose with the sleeve of her jacket. "I found her. I found my mother."

"That's why you're upset? Why you're leaving?"

"No. I mean, yes. No." She leaned her head back and said, "No."

"You're not making any sense. Slow down and tell me what happened."

18

Kate sucked in a sharp breath. "Well, I found my birth mother and her parents, but no one in their house speaks English." Small needles seemed to prick at every inch of her skin as she spoke.

"Your birth mother doesn't even speak English?"

"Actually, she doesn't speak at all." A huge lump formed in her throat and Kate desperately wanted to swallow it, but found it impossible. More tears came unbidden and she buried her face in her hands. Duran continued to hold her tight. When she finally gained her composure, she said, "She lives with her parents, and I really want to find out what happened to her, but it's impossible now. I have to get out of here."

"What happened? You're shaking."

"I ran into Ricco."

"What's he doing here?"

"He was badgering the priest at the church and, and he grabbed me. If some people hadn't come, he'd still have me."

Duran growled. "Did he hurt you? I'll kill him."

Kate patted Duran's chest. "No." Kill him? The idea that Duran was capable of killing someone hit her hard in the chest. "I'm fine. No one is hurting anyone." Which wasn't really true. She could feel a bruise forming on her chest where Ricco's knee had jammed in and the scratches on her fingers still burned.

He pulled her tight again, his hand brushing down her hair. "You're safe now."

"I'll never know what really happened to my mother. How she got here. How she got hurt."

"Did you get your grandparents' phone number?"

She did have it. It was included in the listing she'd found on the Internet. "I have it, but I don't speak Italian. I wouldn't understand what they were saying."

The more she told him about it, the more she wanted to go back and talk to them. A small ounce of hope sprung up in her as she looked at Duran.

"Your dad isn't here with her?"

She shook her head. She couldn't tell him about Vinny. "Not here."

"Wait. You know where he is? Can't you ask him?"

"No." A strangled chuckled came out of her mouth. "I can't ask him."

"Who is it? I'll ask him for you."

"No. I don't want you to ever know who he is."

"Why? Why not? Why can't you tell me?"

"I just can't."

He huffed. "I want to help you, but you're making it very difficult."

He wanted to help. The spot of hope had grown with each passing second. She had to know the whole truth about what happened to her mother. She knew she wouldn't be able to concentrate on anything until she knew. It was all clear in that moment. "Will you come with me to their house? Come with me so I can go home."

He squeezed her tight. "How about you leave on a train immediately, and I go and talk to them in your place. Then I'll call you with the information. You can't stay here, with not only Bellinis everywhere, but Marconis too."

"That would be ideal, but it won't work. They would never trust you or talk to you. They were totally skittish and kept putting their fingers to their lips telling me to be quiet as I left. They're afraid."

"Why?"

Kate looked around as if someone was lurking somewhere waiting for her to tell him so they could pounce on them. "That's the question." She could guess at the answer, but nothing more.

Duran rubbed his hand over his forehead and sighed. "I thought we weren't going to have any more secrets, but you seem to have quite a few you are keeping from me."

She should have known he would hear the secret behind her words. "Not because I don't trust you or want to tell you, but because it puts you in danger to know the little I know. I don't, however, know everything."

"And you want me to just take your word for it?"

"Please. Trust me on this, you don't want to know."

He paced. Someone tried the door. They both froze, listening. Time crawled by as they waited.

He turned to her with resignation in his eyes, "I don't know how to keep you safe here. No. You're going to have to wait."

"I can't. I thought I could. I thought I could go out there and buy a ticket and go be safe, but I can't. I'm going back. I'll use an online translator or something if I have to. I can't not know. And a part of me feels like if I leave, they win. The bad guys win."

She pulled back from him and let the silence fill the room. She could feel the conflict raging inside him.

He moved toward her, shaking his head. "No. I'm going to put you on that train and you are leaving here."

"No you won't. I'll scream."

"You make me crazy." He looked at his watch. "I have to go back to work or they'll be suspicious."

"Who? Who will be suspicious?"

"The people I'm working for."

"The Bellinis? They're family."

"Yes. But the girl I was in charge of escaped."

The words she was going to say got caught in her throat. She was that girl and they had said it was a test for him. "I'm sorry. I'm so sorry."

"For the record, I don't want you to go at all, but I obviously have no control over what you choose to do. I don't like it one bit, but I understand why you want to do this. I can't go right now. I have a few things to do first, and I need to make sure no one is on my tail."

She told him the address and he gave her a route to take. There was a certain gondola service she was to use and specific streets to take from the water.

"I don't get off for two more hours. So it will be at least two and a half before I can get there and that's if no one is watching me."

"Okay. I'll be at their house in two hours and I'll just wait for you." It suddenly occurred to her exactly how much danger she was putting him in. "Wait. I can't ask this of you. Seriously, I'll just use a translator app."

Though he still looked conflicted, he said, "No. I'll go. I'll be careful. No one will see me, but, if I don't show up, that means I couldn't shake the eyes and you have to leave the country immediately. If that happens, we'll find another way to get the information from them. Understand?"

"I don't know."

"Yes you do. You said yourself you need this information." He sucked in a loud breath. "Here. I want you to take this with you." He pulled a knife out of his pocket.

She stepped back. "I'm not taking that. I wouldn't know what to do with it."

"You can and you will if you need to. I'm going to show you how."

She shook her head. While she had been taking daily self-defense classes for the last month, they never used real weapons.

"Don't show you have it until they get close to you. When they do, you strike. Right here, in the gut if you can. Or in a leg, so they're immobilized."

He demonstrated again. She practiced, feeling sick. She didn't want to think about why Duran knew so much about knife fights.

"It took you three seconds to retrieve the knife, so I'm going to show you what that is like when someone attacks you." He took three steps from her. "Now," he said, rushing her. She pulled the knife and it would have been perfect for her to stab him in the chest.

"That was good. Do you see how close they need to be before you reach for it? Only three steps. One, two, three, pull. Stick them immediately, don't hesitate. Don't do it like you're pulling out a gun." Like she knew what it was like to pull a gun. "Move your hand slowly to the knife, then pull it fast. That way they will be caught off guard. And yank the knife back out of them in case you need to stab again."

The thought of actually using the knife made her sicker than ever, but she said, "Thank you," anyway. "Guess who I ran into in Bologna?" She needed to come clean about everything she could.

"I'm not sure I want to know."

"Veronica."

"What?" He jerked forward and grabbed her arms.

"It's okay. She obviously hadn't gotten the memo that I'd escaped. She thought I'd been sent here like everyone else."

"She'll talk, Kate. That's what she does." He ran a hand through his hair. "One more thing we need to worry about. This was today?"

"No. Late last night."

"Well, let's hope she hasn't brought you up in any of her conversations today. This is not good."

"I told her I was leaving Bologna today, and I've been in Venice all day, so maybe if she does tell someone, she'll also tell them I'm not there anymore and she'll forget about me."

"We can only hope." Doubt played on his face. "I'll ask about Ricco, see if he's still around. If someone got him or if he left Venice."

Either way, she was in trouble. If the Bellinis had him, they'd find out she was there. If he left, the Marconis would know or have a second witness if Veronica had already told someone about seeing her. Dizziness swept over Kate and she put her hand on the wall to steady herself. She wanted to tell Duran she was scared, but knew it wouldn't be wise.It was good that she hadn't gone back with Ellie. It would have put her friend in a lot of danger. Kate would have to take a train straight for the airport when she left here. That way she wouldn't risk Veronica making a connection between the three of them. Veronica had only seen Kate at the party, not Ellie or Colby.

"Lock the door behind me and wait at least fifteen minutes before you head for the gondolas. And be careful. Please." Duran pulled her back into a hug and kissed her. When they broke apart he hesitated, brushing her cheek gently with his knuckles as he left.

Kate locked the door and paced the room. Several people tried the door while she waited, making her more nervous. She needed to talk to Ellie. Kate pulled out her phone and dialed, crossing her fingers that her best friend would answer.

"Kate?"

"Yep." Kate held her breath, trying to divert the tears that burned her eyes. What could she say?

"I'm glad you called. I've been so worried."

Kate relaxed, her fears dissipating. "I'm sorry I ditched you. Are you with Colby?" Unable to hold back the tears any longer, Kate sucked in another sharp breath and started to cry.

"He's here, I'm putting you on speaker. What happened? Are you okay? Are you on the train back?"

Kate sniffed several times and forced herself to regain her composure.

"I went to the grave and guess what? My grave was right next to it." She sniffed.

"What?"

"My grave was next to Carmela's, as if my body was in there."

"That must've been awful."

"It was. But, I noticed there were no graves for my grandparents and it got me thinking. What if my grandparents weren't dead either? I could meet them and tell them I was alive."

"Oh no. Kate, listen to me—"

"And I remembered," Kate interrupted her. She didn't want to listen to Ellie try to talk her out of meeting with her grandparents since it was over and done with. Nothing she could do about it now.

"What did you remember?"

"The dream, the one that has been on repeat for last few years, was real. It was a memory. They shot my birth mother while I sat next to her." Kate swallowed hard.

"No. I'm sorry, Kate, you should—"

Kate sucked in a deep breath. "You'll never believe it, but Carmela isn't dead. She's alive, Ellie." Kate whispered it.

"What?"

"I visited her. She can't talk." Kate forced her words out over the lump in her throat. "She's in a wheelchair and can't even move herself. My grandparents don't speak English, but Duran is going to go and interpret for me."

"Wait! You can't just ask him to interpret for you. He said you're in danger and you'll put him in danger too. Besides, if you ask him to help you, you're going to have to tell him the truth about everything. Have you thought of that?"

"I can't. I can't tell him about Vinny. And he's already agreed to do it."

"He's going to find out," Ellie said. Kate could imagine Ellie pacing the room she was in while she talked.

"Not from me." Kate pressed her lips together hard.

"Maybe it should come from you." Ellie's voice was soft, but adamant.

Kate shook her head. "No. No. He can never know." She brushed at her tears with the heel of one of her hands.

"Fine. I know there's no talking you out of anything these days. I'm scared for you, though."

"Can we talk about something else?"

"Okay, guess what?"

"What?"

"Our family is descended from royalty. Kings and queens and all that stuff. We're going to talk our parents into taking us to England next year to go see where our ancestors lived."

"Cool," Kate said. Her mind wandering to her parents in Texas and their secrets. Her nerves rose yet again. "I've got to go. I'll catch the first train out of here after I talk to them. Love you bunches."

"Be careful, Kate. I love you, too."

Colby's voice came over the line. "Kate. Please. Just come back now."

"You know I can't, Colby. But I love you, too."

He exhaled loudly and said, "Right back at atcha."

Kate hung up before they had a chance to argue further. She checked her phone for the library's hours of operation. Twenty-five minutes before they closed. If she hurried, she'd have maybe fifteen minutes to work. She bundled up and got moving.

19

Kate sat down at a computer and pulled up her birth parents' histories. She wanted to find out what kind of people her ancestors were also—on every side of her family. She had found Carmela's parents. It was time to uncover what she could about Abrie's. It was easy to trace back from her dad, Tom, because she knew the names of a lot of his ancestors, but her mom, not so much. It hit her then exactly how strange it was that she knew next to nothing about her adoptive mom's side of the family, only really what she had discussed with her mom at the picnic before she coming to Italy. But she had two names: Piero and Alessa. And perhaps Donati too.

While she worked, a couple of people came in and printed things and then left. Each time she'd flip to the door to see who it was. No luck with Alessa, but she did get several hits with Piero Donati. Was one of these Pieros her adoptive grandfather? Abrie's dad? She became more and more frustrated when each attempt at finding a connection between Piero, Alessa, and Abrie fell through. Since her mom had no brothers or sisters and no contact with her parents, Kate figured they must be dead. But someone had texted her mom in Italy just before she left. Perhaps the secret was that they were alive. If not, she should have been able to find them. Dead people were searchable on Family Search after all.

Kate glanced at the clock. Five minutes left.

She left the Family Search site and put in her adoptive mom's name into the Internet search bar. It appeared that her mom's name, spelled the way she spelled it, was a nickname for Abrielle. An Italian name. No surprise there. Even though she still hoped it wasn't true, she couldn't keep denying the facts. Abrie was Italian.

Kate put the data into the search bar and a slew of names pulled up. Even after she narrowed the search to Italy the number of names was insurmountable. Just as she was about to give up, she recognized two names: Piero and Alessa Donati. Her adoptive mom's parents. Kate's grandparents. She pulled out her phone and looked at the picture of the people on the horse. Were these the people responsible for the deaths of all those people in the pictures? Kate shuddered.

A man entered the room and spoke, but it was in Italian. She looked at the clock on the wall. Closing time. She pressed Print and retrieved the paper from the printer before leaving. The man walked behind her as she made her way out.

Kate walked directly to the place on the canal where Duran had told her to go, the knife in her waistband a constant reminder of the danger she was in and her mind going crazy with the need to investigate the Donatis. The feeling of being watched returned despite her belief that it was impossible. One thing she knew for sure, she couldn't lead her stalker to her birth mother and grandparents. She walked out onto the docking area for the gondola company and rented the entire boat.

While twilight was setting in, the waterways were full of tourists and gondolas as well as some motorboats. Kate couldn't believe she'd only been in Venice for less than a full day. It seemed that day would never end. Duran had been right, the route the gondolier took was not simply along the main drag. He wove in and out of canals, under one bridge after the other until even she was not sure where she was. She was getting antsy, wondering if he would ever dock, but at last he did. She didn't tip him, thinking the fee for the ride was exorbitant as it was, and she was running out of money fast.

She checked the street signs. She was exactly where Duran had told her she would be. Her phone vibrated. Martino. Crap. She'd forgotten about dinner.

Before she even spoke, he did. "Hello. Where can I pick you up?"

Her chest felt tight and all she could think about was lying. Instead, she said, "Shoot, Martino. I'm so sorry. We decided to go to Venice. We thought we'd be back, but unfortunately, we aren't."

There was silence on the other end. Kate tried to apologize again.

"Can we have a rain check for tomorrow? I'm really sorry. I would have called, but things got complicated here."

"I don't think so. I wanted you to meet my family." Was he crazy? Why did he want her to meet his family? Once they found out her real last name, they'd probably see that she was killed or something.

"We could go tomorrow." She didn't know why she kept pushing it. She wasn't going to be there tomorrow night. She'd never see him again.

"The dinner is tonight. Everyone… My mom was expecting you."

"Crap, Martino. I don't know what to say. I can't magic my way to you, as much as I'd like to."

"You should have called." He was being so stiff. Completely inflexible.

"I should have," she conceded. "You're right. Tomorrow? Please?" She was regretting giving him her phone number.

"This must be why Veronica didn't take to you right off. She knew you weren't dependable just laying eyes on you."

"Come on, Martino. That's not fair." She heard whispers in the background and stopped walking, sliding off the main path to hopefully create a quieter space.

"One more minute," the faint female voice said. "We'll have her in one minute."

Martino spoke over the voice, but Kate had heard it anyway. Her heart thumped hard in her chest. Were they talking about her? Had he sent someone to follow her and she was about to be snatched? "I'll tell you another lesson about being Italian." He continued to talk while she jerked her head in all directions looking for someone approaching.

"Italians keep their commitments," he said. "They do what they say they are going to do."

She focused on the quiet voices in the background. "Keep her on. A little longer." On instinct, she hung up. His words echoed in her mind. *Italians keep their commitments. They do what they say they are going to do.*

Was he tracing her call? Is that what had been happening? It had to be. He had been stringing her along yesterday, pretending to still want to meet with her. She had messed it up by being here. No wonder he was cross. He had planned on ambushing her simply because she was a Bellini and he was a Gatti. She hoped she had hung up in time. It didn't really matter, she decided, if they had pinpointed her location. She was on the move and Venice was a big place. She had told Martino she was in Venice. Maybe they were hoping she was in a hotel room right then. Her heart ached just a little thinking about Martino betraying her. She obviously wasn't a good judge of character. Her phone vibrated. She ignored it. Fear reared up in her again. Doubt raged. What was she doing? She was no match for these people.

The heavy feeling of being watched slammed into her. Impossible. Kate stopped at a little park area and sat on one of the benches, hoping someone would be there to help her feel safe if only for a minute, but it was empty. She was cold though the evening was still warm and her mouth felt sandpapery. She startled at every sound, her eyes darting from place to place. She knew she was acting like a victim, but she couldn't help it. Her mind seemed scrambled.

She wanted to get back to her grandparents. She clasped her hands to stop their shaking and stood, hoping that would clear her mind. It didn't. All she could think about was how scared she was that Martino had traced the call and now the Gatti family was about to snatch her. Maybe she could go and get a police escort. She thought over the day and realized she hadn't seen a single cop let alone a police station. She fingered her locket and then huffed. She couldn't stay here all night. She started to walk again, staying in areas that seemed the most well-lit.

Feeling alone with no eyes watching her, she breathed out a sigh of relief and picked up the pace, laughing at herself for being so paranoid. Then out of nowhere, someone grabbed her. She thought of what Duran had taught her, but what could she do now that someone was on her? She didn't have three steps to work with. She called on her self-defense course instead and stomped hard on her attacker's instep. His grip loosened, so she used her elbow to jab him in the gut. He bent over, his grip relaxed some more, but not enough. Desperate, she reached for the knife and pulled it out. She swung at his thigh, making contact and letting the blade sink deep. The man gasped and clutched reflexively at the wound. Kate was sickened by the feel of the knife sinking in, but she didn't let it distract her enough to leave the knife behind. She pulled it back out. The man staggered back.

And she ran.

Duran had been right. She had used it when she had needed to. She ran past her grandparents' home and around the block to the house behind theirs. She crept into the small back yard and climbed over the stone wall. Only then did she allow herself a moment to catch her breath. She leaned on the wall, breathing hard and fast, forcing herself not to cry. She heaved a few times, but didn't throw up. Her knees buckled a little as she stepped from the wall, but after taking another deep breath, she was able to continue walking. She pulled out her phone to call Duran to tell him to forget it, but realized she had no number for him. She needed to tell him about Martino and the attack.

She decided against going through the back door, afraid she'd freak her grandparents out. Instead she unlocked the gate and slinked along the exterior wall to the front door making a mental note to be sure to lock the gate before she left for the night. When she knocked on the door, her grandparents ushered her quickly inside. Before she could pull up a translation app to try to communicate, someone rapped on the door. Her grandparents startled and began talking animatedly to each other. The app popped up and she typed in *friend*. Then she repeated the word, *amico,* several times as she walked toward the door. Both stood up, reaching their hands out to her and shaking their heads. Kate held her hand out, trying to reassure them and repeating, *amico, amico,* until she opened the door and let in Duran.

In a rush, she needed to tell him about Martino and the attack, but she could hear the concerned voices of her grandparents behind her. "They aren't taking your presence well."

He nodded, taking in the scene. "I'll talk to them and calm them down."

He started speaking as he walked slowly toward them. Soon he had her grandma smiling while he held her hands in his. Kate's grandpa had also relaxed. They even did the whole kiss-the-cheek thing. They repeated the word *fidanzato,* looked at Kate, and smiled. Whatever that word was, it seemed to make everything better. The two of them sat back down on the sofa with smiles on their faces. Duran moved toward Kate and took her hand before motioning that she should also sit. "They understand that I'm here to interpret and that I'm no threat. Let's start. What do you want me to ask them?"

"What did you tell them? What does *fidanzato* mean?" She stumbled over the word.

"Boyfriend." He looked quickly away.

Warmth rushed throughout her body. Just the thought of him thinking of calling himself that made her feel like she'd won the lottery. Martino and the attack flew out of her mind. "Everything. Ask them about my parents and me."

He raised an eyebrow.

She bit her lip and stared at him with pleading eyes. "This may be my only opportunity to find this stuff out." Kate turned on the voice recorder on her phone. She didn't want to miss a thing.

Duran nodded and asked her grandparents to tell Kate's parents' story. Then he interpreted, his voice low but clear as her grandmother spoke.

"Your mama loved you and your father. Story of true love at first sight. Her husband had a good job in New York. They were happy. Baby born. You. They cherished you. Everything changed. Shortly after they went back to the States, your grandparents started getting strange phone calls from her and letters about how they were mixed up with bad things. Your grandparents don't know what, but she didn't want you involved with it." Kate's grandma got up and pulled some papers out of a chest. She held out a bundle of letters tied together with ribbon, then set them on the side table. Kate wanted to snatch up the letters, but figured there would be time for that later. "Your mother wanted to get away from that life for you. Your grandparents were so worried. Your grandma was so upset. Then one day, your mother called from a public phone booth and told them she found a way out and everything was going to be okay.

"They didn't hear from her for several weeks. Then they got a message from a priest, telling them that your mother was very hurt because she'd been shot in the head and was in a coma. He wasn't sure she'd live." Her grandma got all choked up as she said this and her grandpa pulled her close. Duran gave Kate a concerned look. "Your grandparents wanted to fly out, but the priest said it was impossible. There was too much danger. He said the bad men who hurt your mother would not hesitate to hurt them too and their daughter was going to need them when she woke up. He said he would get your mother to them in Italy if she lived.

"They followed the priest's instructions exactly and held a funeral, arranging a fake grave for both your mother and you. After a couple of months, your mother arrived and the man with her told them they had to keep her here and care for her; that she had to stay hidden because if the men who shot her knew she was alive, they would come for her and kill her and your grandparents. He also said your mother might not live long, but she's been with them, alive and beautiful for all these years. They were so happy to have their Carmela back, but they felt the hole that came from knowing their Constanzie, you, were gone."

Tears streamed down Kate's face. "Why?" Kate said. "Why did they shoot her?"

Her grandpa spoke then. "She was telling the authorities about the bad things they were doing and the people they worked for found out." Duran coughed.

"So she was a nark?" he blurted and then gave Kate a confused look. She blanched, but nodded. Her chest felt tight, her breath bottled up inside. Duran's face went slack. Then her grandma spoke and Duran continued to interpret, his voice halting and unsure now. He stared at Kate, sympathy thick on his face.

"You made her see the evil they had gotten wrapped up in and she didn't want that for you. She was brave, reaching for more. She chose good over evil and that will be well with her in the end. God has open arms for her. Your grandparents are proud.

"The priest told them you'd been killed. And yet, you are here. You look as she did at your age. Lovely. They know you are excited about finding your mother, but you cannot tell anyone. Anyone but this sweet boy."

Kate turned to Duran and gave him a look.

"I'm only repeating what they are saying." He smirked, but the smirk didn't remain long. He was obviously making connections Kate didn't want him to make. "Just as I told you they would, they want you to stay so they can care for you, too."

Her grandparents stopped talking and it was Kate's turn to speak while Duran interpreted her words. "I can't. I wish I could. I'm so sorry. I have a family in the States. I was adopted. If things change…if the danger passes, I will return."

Her grandpa spoke. "Your mother wanted a better life. Always knew it was a risk. She wanted to come back here and be close to them again. They feel blessed to have her."

Kate moved back to Duran, tears filling her eyes.

"They have taken you into their memory and will remember every bit about you. Every last detail until you return. And your mother. She sees you. She knows you even though it seems she doesn't. Those men destroyed her life as she knew it, but she is a fighter. She is in there."

The tears kept coming and Duran took her into his arms, holding her tight until she calmed down. He checked the time.

"I hate to leave," he whispered into her ear, "but I really have to go."

She nodded into his shoulder. "I understand." She pulled back and they stood staring at each other for several moments. He spoke to her grandparents and hugged and kissed their cheeks in farewell. Kate took his hand and they walked to the kitchen. "I told them I had to leave and that you should wait a little bit and then go out the back way."

She nodded. "I don't want you to go."

"I know, but I have to. You can move on. We both have to move on. Whether we want to or not."

"I love you, Duran." The words popped out and there was no way for her to take them back.

It surprised her when he said, "I love you too, Kate." He looked her in the eyes and she knew it wasn't something he said as a reaction to her words. He truly felt it. He pulled her close again and spoke into her hair. "I don't like how familiar this all sounds."

"You mean about my mother?" She hoped he hadn't made the connection with Vinny.

He nodded.

"I know." And out of nowhere, a thought came to her mind. "Wait!" She pulled back from him and walked into the living room.

"The priest," she said. "Did he tell you his name?" Duran translated again.

"*Sì!*" Her grandma got up and dug through the pile of papers from the chest until she pulled out a light green one. It looked scarily familiar and Kate rushed to her bag and pulled out her own faded lime green sheet, her hand trembling. Her grandma perused the paper in her own hand and called out, "*Ach!*" and said a bunch of stuff in Italian and then set it back into the chest. She turned to her husband and spoke to him.

"They can't remember his name, but if she heard it, she would recognize it."

"That paper. Can I see it?" Kate stepped closer.

Her grandma pulled it back out of the chest and held it out. Kate took it and held it next to the one she'd found in the attic with her baby things. The paper that Kate believed was written by the man who had saved her from the mafia when she was three. The handwriting on her grandma's green paper matched the writing on hers, but the signature at the bottom was clearer: Angelo Marchesi She handed her grandma's paper back and put her hand to her mouth, the other paper shaking in her other hand.

"What is that?" Duran said, moving toward her.

"Nothing," Kate said in a rush. "I thought it was something, but it wasn't." She put the note back in her bag.

"No secrets," he said. She stopped and held her note out to him, her face burning. Duran began reading the note aloud.

"*Here is the information you requested, Savino—*"

Her grandmother called out and repeated Savino a couple of times.

"Savino—" her grandmother called out, and said something else before she repeated Savino a couple more times.

"What did she just say?"

"She said that the priest's name was Savino." He kept reading. "'Constanzie. Southern Ocean County Hospital.' I'd say this was something. Where did you get this?" Duran shook her note in front of her. She saw betrayal written all over his face.

"It was in my parents' attic."

Her grandfather stood up and took hold of Duran's arm, speaking to him sharply. Duran's voice was steady as he replied, then he turned toward Kate.

"They were afraid I was going to hurt you. I won't. Can we move back into the kitchen or something?"

She nodded and led the way.

"Why do you keep stuff from me?" He looked disappointed. "Is this you, Constanzie?"

"I was afraid to tell you. I thought the signature on the bottom was a Marconi, but I was wrong. That's why I went after your uncle. I needed answers."

He stopped.

"What is your mother's last name?"

She didn't say anything. He repeated the question with a sterner tone. "What is your mom's last name?"

"Bellini." She whispered it.

He shook his head. "You're a Bellini?"

She nodded.

"And you've known since Jersey?"

She nodded. "And your dad? It's Vinny, isn't it? It was the picture. The painting in his office tipped you off."

She nodded again, this time pressing her lips into a straight line.

"His beloved Carmela is your mother." She figured he was picturing the painting, a beautiful woman and the face plate underneath that read, *My Carmela*. She stared at him, her eyebrows scrunching together. "Don't be mad."

"Does Vinny know?"

She nodded. He huffed.

"He tried to protect me when he found out," she blurted, "but he was limited in what he could do."

"That's why he saved you. I wondered. It all makes a lot more sense now." He looked sad. Worn out. "I can even understand why you thought you had to keep it from me, but I won't lie, it hurts that you didn't trust me. And that you obviously still didn't trust me even after knowing what I did for you."

"I was trying to protect you."

"I get it. I do. But it hurts." His shoulders hunched over.

"I'm so sorry. Do you know this Angelo Marchesi?" Kate tapped the signature on her grandma's green notepaper.

Duran nodded. She could hear her grandparents speaking in hushed tones in the living room.

"Who is it?"

"A guy in a competing family, but he's been gone for a while."

Kate's mind whirred. At least that mystery had been solved. A real name to a real person. No longer would she have to wonder who the middleman was that worked with Cremashci. "So, now there's no Cremashci and there's no Angelo. Who helps people like my mother now? Who helps people like me?"

"What are you talking about?"

"Cremashci, the priest."

"I know him. He was my priest, until Alzheimer's took him."

"Yes." She didn't want to go into the details with him now. "He saved all kinds of people from the mafia. He was the one who arranged my escape and my mother's."

"Then why is Marchesi's name on these papers?"

"He must have been the go-between. Savino Cremashci gave to me to Angelo Marchesi, who gave me to my parents in Dallas. And it appears he also got my mother back to her parents, but now there is no one." Kate shook her head and looked at her grandparents. Her grandma was leaning on her grandpa's shoulder. They seemed happy, content. She had brought them that contentment.

"Do you think someone has replaced Cremashci? Do you think he had someone he was training to take his place? Marchesi too?"

"It's not our concern. Forget about it." Duran's face was hard.

"I can't."

"You can. You have to."

"I need to speak with Cremashci." Kate's mind was spinning. She had to make sure both men had successors. There had to be a way to help people on the mafia's hit list.

"No. You don't."

"I can speak with Cremashci and take over for him if he doesn't have a successor. Maybe he can slip me in and help me take his place if there isn't anyone else."

"Can you hear yourself? That's crazy talk. Cremashci has Alzheimer's."

"Yes. I'll talk to him," she continued, ignoring Duran's protests, lost in the excitement of a fresh direction to take. "Then, you can turn me in to Vinny or something so I can be in the thick of things. I can work from the inside. Not at first, but I'll build up to it."

"No. Way." His words sounded final. "That's never going to happen."

"I can't just stand by while people get hurt. And we could be together." She raised an eyebrow.

"Be together? It won't work." Duran scoffed. "And how are you going to come back?"

"I'm not sure yet, but I'll figure it out. I'll talk to Vinny." She pressed her lips together like she was thinking hard.

"No. If you think they are going to let you back into the family, you're crazy."

"I'll tell them I was taken by the FBI and I want to come back, come home." She waggled her eyebrows. "They'll love that."

"Yes, they will, because they'll have found you and will shoot you on sight."

20

"No. They won't do that," Kate said. "I'm a Bellini." She looked at her grandparents.

"Have you forgotten how you ran at the airport? Have you forgotten what they did to your mother and what they planned to do to you?"

Her face went cold. The memory of fighting off Galtem, one of the Marconi goons at the airport, left a bitter taste in her mouth. She sucked in a sharp breath, remembering Ricco on top of her only a short while ago. Duran stared at her, but continued.

"Yeah. I know all about it. You ran. Had you not run and the FBI took you screaming and kicking, it would be a different story. No. There is no return for you."

Kate bit her lip. She knew he was right on one level, but there had to be a way.

"They've most surely tracked you to where you are staying in Bologna and are waiting for your return. Veronica has to have talked by now, and I guarantee it won't take long for her to find out the family didn't send you here. I'm betting she already knows."

"Impossible." Kate was suddenly hugely just glad that Veronica hadn't seen her with her friends. Then she remembered Martino. He'd seen both Colby and Ellie at the party.

"Did you take a taxi while you were there?"

"No. We had a driver."

Duran threw his head back in frustration. "Let me guess. His last name was Marconi."

"How did you…" Kate covered her mouth and then said, "Colby! Ellie! Do you think they've hurt them?" She grabbed out her phone and started to dial Ellie.

Duran snatched it from her. "If they have, they're waiting for your call. They'd have her phone."

"I'll block the number so they can't see it's me." She took her phone back and dialed. When Ellie answered, Kate could hear loud music playing in the background. Her heart slowed its hammering. "You at a party? Not at the house? You're safe?"

"Yes."

"Have you noticed anyone following you?"

"Wait, what? I can't hear." Kate heard shuffling and brushing noises. A door shut and Ellie said, "What did you say?"

"Have you noticed anyone following you?"

"Following me? No."

"Don't go back to the apartment. The Marconis know I'm here and they might know where I've been staying."

"What? The Marconis found us?"

"Most likely. Long story." Kate brushed a hand through her hair. Neither Ellie nor Colby was going to like what she had to say. "In any case, you shouldn't go back to the apartment just in case."

"I'll have Colby and the guys check everything out before we let anyone go back in there. Don't worry."

"No. I don't want you to check it out," Kate's voice got a little shrill. "I want you to stay far away from there."

"Where are we supposed to go? I mean all our…"

"To a hotel," Kate interrupted. "A friend's. Anywhere but there. Just be safe, Ellie. Keep everyone safe. And whatever you do, don't use our driver to get you there." She would call Johansen as soon as she hung up.

"Shouldn't we just call the police?"

"We can't just call the cops in Bologna, not when the Marconis own the town." She'd seen how powerful the Bellinis had been in Jersey. They owned the police there. She was sure the Marconis had the same power in Bologna. "I'll have to try Johansen again and see if he knows any cops we can trust. Let me know where you end up. Don't let Colby or any of his friends go back to that apartment until it is searched." Kate looked at her grandparents who now had worried expressions on their faces.

"Okay."

"I've got to go. Be safe. Please."

"No worries. We'll go to a hotel. Bye."

Kate scowled. "I have to do something, Duran. I have to. Look at what they are doing to my friends. To you. To them." She looked away from her grandparents who were staring at Kate and Duran now. She grabbed Duran's hand and moved back into the kitchen.

"I'll tell you what you are going to do." Duran grabbed both her arms and turned her around to face him. "You are going to go home, finish high school with amazing grades and then you are going to go to college to become an attorney, just like Vinny suggested. Instead of being a defense attorney, you are going to become a prosecutor. Then you are going to use proper channels to bring down the mafia and all its appendages."

"That will take too long and they'll probably find me before then."

"Maybe, but it's the only way you are going to be able to do anything about the mafia without getting killed as soon as you arrive in the States."

He was right. She was only one girl. One girl without any resources. "There has to be a faster way. What about all the people who need to get out now, that have had their lives threatened?"

"They are just going to have to wait until DA Ham...I mean DA, whatever you're going to change your name to, because you have to change your name, comes to town and frees them. I can't believe you haven't already changed your name. I can't believe they haven't found you already."

"They never knew my last name as far as I know. My ticket was to Dallas but we live a little over two hours outside of there. Besides, Special Agent Johansen is watching out for me, too. Come back with me."

"It won't work. If I come with you, we'll just both end up dead sooner. For now, you change your name and go to school, and I continue doing what is expected of me."

"Please." Kate slouched forward, pleading.

"I can't do that. Do you know what would happen to Vinny? If I disappear now it would reflect poorly on him and his bid for head of the family. Believe me that would not be a good thing for anyone. When Vinny ascends to the throne, I'm hoping things are going to get a lot better in mafia land." He looked at her, deep in her eyes and she had to look away. "Kate. I need you to promise me you will go to school and become a prosecuting attorney. That you will stay away from the Bellinis and all things mafia until you have the power to make a difference."

She looked away.

"Kate."

"It's so long. I can't promise…"

"Yes. Yes, you can and you will or I'll just turn you into Vinny today."

"Do it."

Duran growled. "Stop it. I didn't go through everything I did in Jersey just to have you get killed."

"Fine. School. D.A. But, if something sure comes along—"

"It won't. Now, I'm out of here." He looked at his watch and swore. "It's already midnight."

He kissed her, his hands running down her back, leaving a trail of fireworks as they went. He reached for the door. "Oh, and take a water taxi to the train. Don't leave for twenty to thirty minutes, okay?"

He returned to her and pulled her close. He motioned toward the knife still in her waistband. "And keep this close." His eyes rounded as he looked down at the blood spotting her clothing. "You're bleeding."

She followed his gaze, only now realizing what he was talking about. "No. It's not my blood." Memories of the feel of the knife entering her attacker's body filled her and her mouth went dry, her stomach immediately feeling queasy.

"Well, whose blood is it?"

"Some guy who tried to grab me."

"What?" Duran threw his hands wide and took a step back. "And when were you going to tell me about this?"

"Sorry. I—I." She didn't know what to say.

He grabbed her and held her, squeezing her tight, almost too tight. "Why didn't you tell me?" He looked her straight in the eye.

"I wanted to after it happened and really, it sounds stupid, but I forgot once you came in and started talking to my grandparents. I have no idea who it was."

He pulled her tight again, her face snuggled into that sweet spot right under his shoulder. "You're going to have to stay here tonight. I don't dare have you go anywhere."

"I can't stay here. You said yourself that I'll put my family in danger by being here. Whoever it was, they are long gone. In the hospital. Besides, Martino traced my call earlier." She looked at her phone. "They're most likely already here looking for me. I've got to get out of here. I should go straight to the airport here for sure. No Bologna for me."

"Who is Martino?"

"Martino Gatti."

Duran's muscles tensed. "You've got to be kidding me."

"No. And he knows I'm a Bellini."

"That's three groups after you: Gattis, Bellinis, and Marconis. This couldn't be worse. The Gattis are very dangerous. Okay, we'll go with your plan. You go straight to the airport. If someone was sent to snatch you and were unsuccessful, they will send someone else. Guaranteed."

"But the Gattis don't know where I went after the trace. I can still get out of here and keep my grandparents safe. I'm just not sure where to go to catch the train and stay hidden."

Duran was silent for a few seconds, obviously thinking. "I'll tell you what. I'll leave and go show my face at home. Find out if it was a Bellini who was following you. Then I'll sneak back out and double back to keep guard over you. Give me a good half hour. You go out the back door, through the neighbor's backyard. When you get to the street, turn right and head straight for the water. Walk along the edge until you find a water taxi. Take it to the train station. I'll be in the background watching you, making sure you make it safely. You get the heck out of Italy. Don't use the Marconi airport."

She nodded.

"Please don't take this the wrong way," he said. "But I better not get this close to you again until you're that prosecutor, taking them down. Promise me."

"I'm a terrible promise keeper, but I can tell you this, I will take them down."

"You cannot return to the Bellinis or Marconis."

She nodded. Duran hugged and kissed her one last time and then he whispered into her ear, "I love you, Kate Hamilton. Stay alive," and he was gone, out the back door.

Kate was numb as she moved back to the living room and sat down next to her grandparents, pulling a chair close. She showed them pictures of her life in Texas. That she had a happy life. She pointed to and named her family members and using an online translation tool, she explained their relationship to her, keeping an eye on the clock as she did.

When fifteen minutes had passed, she wished she'd asked Duran to tell her grandparents her goodbyes before he left. Now she had no Italian words. Instead she hugged them. They kissed her on both cheeks. Then she asked to see her mother. Kate followed her grandma into her mom's room and Kate kissed Carmela on the forehead before giving her a hug. "I'll miss you, Mom. I'll pray for you, and I hope we can be together again one day. I love you." A hard ball of anger at the unfairness of everything seemed to slam her in the chest as she kissed her mother one last time before leaving out the back door.

Kate wiped at the tears that streamed down her cheeks as she locked the gate and jumped the back wall again. Her mind churned with dark gray and black thoughts. Revenge ravaged through her blood and her mind worked overtime to find a way to get back at the Marconis and Bellinis sooner than the twenty-year plan Duran had espoused. The only way she could think of was to help those marked for death, for whatever reason, to escape that life. She kept circling around to that idea, but no solution presented itself.

Kate took in a heavy breath and for the first time was truly aware of her surroundings. She felt the darkness press on her and the feeling she was not alone hit her. Her eyes darted from side to side. Was she being paranoid? No one was around, but she couldn't shake the feeling of eyes on her as she walked along the road, heading for the water taxis. She could see the water. Should she run? Then she thought of Duran. It had to be Duran. He was the one watching her. She turned the corner at the water's edge, but no water taxis were there. She heard something and whipped around. She screamed as arms encircled her and a hand with a cloth covered her mouth and nose, stifling her scream and making her head go fuzzy. She tried to maneuver her pinned hands to her waist to grab her knife, but she couldn't think anymore. She was so tired and only a moment later she was out.

21

Kate woke in a frilly, girly room. Soft and hard hues of purple and yellow surrounded her. She jolted upright and grabbed at her waist. The knife was gone. She searched her pockets for a phone that was no longer there. Pictures of horses, a young girl, and a young girl playing on the beach, decorated the walls. Kate pushed the large, soft stuffed animals off the bed as she swung her legs off and hopped down, running to the window. She shoved it up, happy to find it opened without any great effort. When she looked out and saw the waves crashing onto the sheer edge of the cliff hundreds of feet below, vertigo set in and she immediately pulled back. The house practically hugged the cliff's edge, and she must have been three levels up. What was going on?

She passed a white desk and scrambled to the door, completely prepared to find it locked. When she turned the doorknob and yanked, the door jerked open. Kate peered out. No one was standing guard. "Huh," the sound slipped out of her mouth as she moved down the hall. "Not very good kidnappers," she murmured to herself. She walked down the hall, taking little, quick steps and then hurried down a grand staircase. This was a home. Whose home? Clanking and voices, the sounds of people eating breakfast filled the hall. She moved toward the sounds, peeking around the corner when she got to the entryway. Six or eight people sat at a long, wooden farm table. Her kidnappers. She'd steal away before they even had a chance to finish their fancy meal.

Kate crossed through the large living room and into a wide open reception area. The front doors stood only fifteen feet from her. Freedom was at her fingertips. She rushed to the grand double doors and swung one open. A part of her still expected it to be locked, but it wasn't. The wide cement porch supported ten large columns, and she gasped as she looked out over the circular drive and the tree lined approach that seemed to go on for miles. Several moments passed before she could get her feet to move down the steps and onto the drive. She didn't run, but walked at a rapid pace instead. She had a long way to go.

After about ten minutes, she heard the distant sound of horses' hooves on the ground. Not looking back, she kept on a forward path, her heart thumping hard from her expended effort and the fear rising in her gut. An older lady atop a tall horse crossed fifteen feet or so in front of her a stopped, a second horse trailing behind, and stopped. When a rider on a horse went up against someone not on a horse, the rider always won.

"Hello."

Kate did not stop or acknowledge the lady, she kept moving forward past the horse. Perhaps the horses and the lady would disappear if she pretended not to see them.

"It's six kilometers to the gate, so I brought along a horsey friend you can use."

"Six kilometers?" Kate stopped and huffed, letting her arms go stiff at her sides so they wouldn't shake. She would not show fear. She refused to look at the lady. "Where are we?"

"Why, Italy, my dear."

Kate rolled her eyes and started to walk again. The lady walked her horse beside Kate.

"I'm not your dear. I don't know who you are, but you can't just take people off the streets and hold them prisoner. I want to go home." Beads of sweat formed on her hairline, and she brushed them away with a swipe of her arm.

"Even the crazy Italian police would be hard pressed to consider a grandmother a kidnapper. Especially when the person she allegedly kidnapped was in so much danger."

Kate stopped in her tracks and looked at the lady on the horse. She had long, wavy brown hair, and a vibrant aura surrounding her, completely unlike an old grandmother.

"That's right, take a good look."

Kate glanced quickly away and clenched her jaw, fear rising in her gut. "What are you talking about?" Kate couldn't deny that the lady's voice did sound familiar despite the obvious Italian accent. Was she Vinny's mom? The woman didn't look anything like Vinny and Kate had already met Carmela's parents.

"I'm sure you caught the resemblance. I'm your grandmother Donati, Kate."

Pictures shuffled through her mind. Pictures of a cute couple on a horse. Pictures of mangled and dead bodies. Kate couldn't help it, she screamed, turned, and ran as fast as she could toward the gate. She heard the horses hooves hit the pavement behind her. Kate ran faster, but she wasn't fast enough. The woman turned the horse in front of Kate, jumped down, and grabbed Kate. Kate screamed again and jerked away from the woman. "Murderer!" she yelled. "Murderer!"

"I have no idea what you are talking about. You have nothing to fear from me."

"Alessa Donati? You are Alessa Donati? You admit it?"

"Of course I admit it."

"I saw the pictures. You disgust me. I am not your granddaughter."

"I don't know what pictures you are talking about, Kate. Why don't you fill me in?"

"The picture my mom, your daughter, has of you and Piero. The pictures of the all those dead people."

Alessa sighed. "Yes, Piero was my husband, but whatever your mom told you about us and those dead people, it simply isn't true."

"You're saying you had nothing do with those murders? Those pictures?"

"I have no idea what pictures you're talking about, but this I can tell you: your grandfather and I never, never killed anyone. If I'd have known that's what your mother thought all this time, I would have set her straight." Now that Kate was talking and no longer struggling to get free, Alessa's arms relaxed and fell away.

Kate looked at this self-assured woman. Really looked. She did have some characteristics very similar to her mom. Her light skin color, her dark blue eyes and perfectly shaped ears. This really was her mom's mother, the woman in the picture on the horse. "I don't understand." Kate was sure she looked a bit crazy after her quick departure from the house. Still, she lifted her chin high, unwilling to appear weak.

"I'm sorry Abrielle led you to believe we were murderers. We were not and I continue not to be."

"She didn't tell me. I found the pictures. Your picture was the first one in the stack. The only one with people who were alive."

"I think it's about time I spoke with your mom even if she has no desire to. I need to see those pictures and maybe we can come to an understanding. No wonder she hates me so much."

"There were names on the backs of some of the pictures. I took pictures of the names."

"We'll have to take a look. I'm certain Abrielle won't talk to me over the phone, so maybe it's time for a trip to the States. Then again, she did text me and tell me to stay away from you while you were here." Kate raised an eyebrow. "Until then, I ask you to give me the benefit of the doubt. Innocent until proven guilty, if you please."

"She told you to stay away from me?"

"She did, but now at least I have an idea why. Her text, however, made me concerned and I was determined to find you and watch out for you, which I did."

"I don't understand," Kate repeated, looking at her hands and poking her tongue hard into her cheek. She kept swallowing, unable to get any moisture in her mouth. This was not happening.

"I know. Why don't you hop on this horse and we'll talk as we head to the gate, and if by the time we get there, you still want to run away, I'll call you a cab. Heavens, I'll drive you to the nearest airport myself."

"You took my phone." Kate's body temperature rose and her chest tightened.

"I did." Her grandmother hopped off her horse. "I didn't want you doing something foolish, like calling your mother and frightening her needlessly."

"But, I-I ..."

"I'll give you back your phone as soon as you make the decision to stay or go. Now, hop on Tesorina here. She's a good horse."

"I've never ridden a horse before." Kate took a step backward and clasped her hands together.

"No? I would have thought your mom would have at least passed that little nugget onto you."

"My mom rode horses?" The heat inside Kate felt had built to a fever pitch. Who was her mom anyway?

"Oh, yes. And she was quite good at it. But, no worries, Tesorina here is as gentle as they come." Kate did not step toward the horse. "I have a lot to teach you if you'll let me. Riding a horse is one of the easier things." Her grandmother demonstrated how to mount the horse. "I'll help you if you need it. Use that boulder next to Tesorina to help you up."

Kate stepped forward—what else could she do?—and followed the directions. She shocked herself by getting on the horse on her first try.

"Excellent."

Feeling like she'd really done something amazing, Kate smiled, her frustration and confusion melting away.

"Now," her grandma said. "I know you feel unsure right now, and Tesorina is pretty good about that kind of thing, but you need to learn to take command of the horse and make it feel like you are confident and in control even when you don't feel it deep down."

She directed Kate how to make the horse move one way or the other. "If Tesorina starts to trot, pull back gently on the reins. If she starts to run, same thing, only slowly increase the strength of the pull until she slows back down. Panic will get you nowhere. That being said, it's highly unlikely Tesorina will try to take off, I just want you to be prepared if something spooks her."

Her grandma hopped on top of her own horse.

"Now," Kate said, as they headed for the ranch gates, "tell me about my mom." It was hard to imagine her proper mom, Abrie, riding a horse.

"Well, I'm sure at this point you know much more about who she is now than I do, but when she was born, she changed our lives. We wanted to do everything for her. She was so beautiful, and we loved her very much. She made our lives joyful. We lived here and had a wonderful life. Then your grandpa got a wild hair to go to America. He felt he'd conquered Italy and wanted to conquer a new country." A shadow seemed to cross her grandmother's face, but it left as quickly as it'd come. "So we left on our new adventure and it turned out to be harder than he anticipated, and more ruthless than he'd ever dreamed. He worked hard and did what he had to in order to survive."

"Like killing people?"

"No." Her tone was firm. "There were some Italian families who were not kind and gentle like your grandfather, but they were prospering and your grandfather got caught up in it all. At first he wanted to change things and did, but not enough. My sons—"

"Wait a minute," Kate interrupted. "I have uncles?" This was too much. Sensing her distress Tesorina sped up, coming close to a trot. Kate loosened the pressure she'd added to the horse's sides and their pace began to settle down.

"Of course you have uncles."

"Do I have any aunts?" Kate was starting to feel light-headed.

"Unfortunately no, but you do have two uncles."

"In America?" Tesorina finally slowed. Their pace wasn't much faster than walking, but at least Kate wasn't doing the walking.

"One stayed in America when I returned. The other is here in Italy. It appeared that your grandpa was making headway with the Italian families, but in reality, he kept hitting setback after setback. Piero, however, was no quitter. Unfortunately, he started taking part in the nonsense that was going on. The people he was working with were his countrymen after all. I didn't approve, but I loved that man. Your mom also didn't approve, and wanted me to leave America and go back home to Italy. I wasn't about to leave your grandpa, though. I stayed until he was killed."

Kate gasped.

"Yes. He was killed by a competing family. My sweet husband was dead, and I was heartbroken. By that time, your mom had already run away."

Despite her confusion, Kate suddenly noticed the fresh scents in the air: newly mown grass, the fragrances of various flowers and something else earthy. She took in a deep breath, finally relaxing.

"When I refused to come back here with your mom, she disappeared. Ran away. She was seventeen. Your age. It broke your grandfather's heart. It broke mine. I found her after your grandfather was killed. By that time, she was happily married and didn't seem to notice we weren't a part of her life anymore. Now I understand why she was so eager to leave."

"Why didn't you find her earlier?" Kate's question came more out of curiosity than as an accusation.

"She made it clear in the note she left us that she didn't want us to bother her. We had to honor that. I despaired when your grandfather was murdered. Your two uncles took over the business, which was booming and that was probably why they killed him. I couldn't deal with any of it. I came back here. Alone. It took me a couple of years to come out of my depression. Part of the reason I was able to move on was because I'd finally found your mom. Seeing her be so successful and happy made me have the confidence I needed to continue on with my life."

They rode in silence for a little while, the clopping of the horses' hooves on the asphalt soothing.

"What do you want from me?" Kate said, noticing the large iron gate was getting closer and closer. She needed to make her decision about this woman in the next few minutes.

"I want to have a relationship with you." She smiled at Kate, warm and seemingly free of pretense.

"But, you know I'm adopted, right?" She hated how uncertain she sounded when she said it.

Her grandmother nodded and they stopped only a few meters from the gate.

"Of course I do. Despite that, you are my granddaughter."

"But my mom left." Kate rubbed at her forehead.

"Yes, and she won't like me talking to you." Her grandmother pressed her lips together sternly.

"Are you doing this to get back at her?"

"Oh, no. I'm afraid my reasons are just as selfish, however. From what I've seen, you're an amazing young woman and I'd like to get to know you. I have no desire to hurt your mom."

"So, if I decided to go right now, you'd let me?" Kate stared at the gate and only then discovered the guard shack and the large man inside it, watching them.

"Yes, but I hope you'll decide to stay."

Kate considered her grandmother's words. "What if I want to leave in a few hours?" Kate's horse chuffed.

"Then you may."

"If I go back and get my phone and bag and want to leave, I can?" Kate couldn't keep the uncertainty out of her voice. This woman had kidnapped her. Was it all a ruse just to keep her calm until they could secure her?

"Listen, Kate. You can leave whenever you want to. I'm not keeping you here. You are free to go. Of course, I'll have to help you leave the country safely if that's what you choose to do. You certainly can't stay in Italy without some protection."

There was something in her grandma's voice that told Kate she was speaking the truth. "What if I want my friends to come here?"

"They may come. I'd love to meet your friends. Why weren't they with you?"

"I sent them away because…" Kate stopped, feeling silly for not realizing the truth of what she'd done.

"Because you knew you were in danger?"

Kate nodded, her face blanching as she thought of abandoning Ellie. "And my mom. Can I call my mom?"

"You may. You may not like what she has to say, but yes, you may call her. This is the moment to decide what you want to do for you. You're old enough to decide by yourself." She stressed the "yourself".

"I'll go back to the house. I need to talk to my friends and my mom." While determined and even a bit eager to talk to them, she couldn't help but worry about what they might say or do.

"Wonderful. We'll have a bit of time to get to know each other on the way back."

22

At the house, Kate slid off Tesorina's back with all the grace of a drunk grizzly bear, and landed on her bum. Her grandma, on the other hand, hopped off as if she rode every day, which she undoubtedly did.

As Kate stood and brushed herself off, a man came around the side of the house and led the horses away like he'd been waiting for just this very thing. It occurred to Kate for the first time that her grandma was extremely wealthy. In turn, didn't that make her mom really wealthy? No. She'd left that life. Kate stared at the back of her grandma as they climbed the front steps, studying her light olive skin, her lean and well cared for physique. Until she turned her dark blue eyes on Kate, at which point, Kate looked quickly away as if she hadn't been looking at all. It struck Kate at that moment how much of her grandma her mom had inherited. "Wait a minute," Kate said, hopping up the steps two at a time. "Those pictures in the room I slept in, those are of my mom, aren't they?"

"Indeed. Wasn't she a doll?"

Kate chuckled. "So all of this was yours before you left for the States?"

Her grandmother nodded.

"But, who took care of it while you were gone?"

"Our whole staff stayed on to run the ranch. It was your grandfather's pride and joy and he would never have abandoned it."

"And yet, you never came back to visit it while you were in America?"

Her grandmother snorted. "Not for seven years. I figured your grandfather was afraid that if we came for a visit, we'd never return. And, he would have been right in that assumption."

"So what did he do to be able to have this ranch?"

"He was in textiles if you can believe that."

They walked into the house and Kate couldn't help but notice the beautiful tapestries, rugs and drapes decorating the main room.

"He sold items to the Vatican, the Russian Prime Minister, the German Chancellor... In any case, he was not only great at what he did, he loved it."

"He must have been good if it produced this." Kate looked around in awe as they walked toward the kitchen. She'd missed everything on her way out.

"Yes. He had a gift for creating relationships with people. One of my sons, your uncle Tomasso, inherited that gift and he took over the business when your grandfather died. Your other uncle, Ernesto takes care of the empire in the States."

They crossed into the massive kitchen.

"And had my mom stayed?"

"Well, your mom, she wasn't much of a business woman. I'm sure she would have found her own path, most likely with the ranch. She loved the animals, and she loved the ranch hands. She was a people person, much like your grandpa, just never had the stomach for *making the deal.*"

Kate's pride in her mom ratcheted up several notches and she stood taller and smiled. "She has a hyper sense of right and wrong, you mean?"

Her grandma nodded, opened the fridge and pulled out a glass pitcher of water and set it on the counter. "It's a rare thing."

"I don't know," Kate said. "I don't think it's really that rare. I think we all have that thing inside us, that guide that makes us feel bad when we do or are about to do something that is bad. That is the indicator for right or wrong, I think."

"Yes," her grandma said as she pulled out two tall glasses from the cupboard. "But, do most choose to listen to that guide?"

"*Touché.*" Kate said, noticing her phone next to a laptop on the large farm table. She glanced at her grandmother who was pouring the water.

"Go right ahead. It's fully charged and the laptop is for your use also." There was a pause before she asked, "Does your family still attend church?" She sounded inquisitive rather than accusatory.

"Yep."

"And?"

"I like church. I like my priest. Sure it can get boring sometimes, but there's something there that makes me feel right somehow."

"Something here," her grandma said, placing her open palm over her heart.

"Yeah. Just like that." Kate's hand went to her heart too before she reached out and picked up her phone and noticed Duran's knife was also there on the table. The metal shone in the light.

Her grandma nodded and walked toward her with two glasses of water. "You and I are going to get along just fine. As for your knife, I had one of my men clean it up for you. I'm glad it wasn't one of them you decided to stab."

Kate shuddered. "It was awful." She opened and closed her hand, a shiver grabbing onto her spine.

"But necessary. You did what you had to do. I understand."

"Wait. How did you even know about that?"

"I had someone tailing you."

"You too? Creepy. Why? Why were you following me?" Kate tore her eyes away from the knife and picked up her phone.

"Let's just say I know things."

"No. You don't get away with saying that. How did you know?"

"I know you're anxious to make some calls, so I'll leave you to it. Oh, and your bag is upstairs in your room if you need it. At lunch, I'd very much like to hear what's been going on with you. And you can show me the pictures if you'd like." Wow, now Kate knew how her mom got so good at avoiding answering questions. Apparently that was a family trait. Her grandmother set the glass on the table next to Kate before moving quietly away. Kate would have to be okay with not having the answer right then. She grabbed the water and took a drink as she made her way to an overstuffed leather sofa in the room adjacent to the kitchen. She set the glass on a coaster on the side table and settled in.

Her phone clicked on and as she'd anticipated, she had a ton of text and voice messages. Kate smiled despite herself. It was nice to have someone who cared about her enough to worry about her. Instead of checking the messages, she just called Ellie. It was easier that way.

The phone rang, but Ellie never picked up. The call went straight to voicemail. Strange. Ellie never let her phone die. Never. Kate listened as the message played. "Hey! This is Ellie! I'm in Italy so you're just going to have to wait to talk to me. Get over it." Kate blew a puff of air out of her nose. That message was the epitome of Ellie.

Kate called Colby with the same result. What was going on? Fear raced through her veins. What if Veronica had them? Kate quickly pulled up the texts.

Ellie: We got a couple hotel rooms for everyone. The guys are dying to go by the apartment. I'm not sure I'll be able to stop them.

Ellie: Okay. I can't stop them. They are going to go see what they can see.

Ellie: Are you there? What's happening? The guys are watching the apartment and it's kinda freaky.

Hope you're okay.

Ellie: OMG Kate! Someone just went into the apartment. Some man.

Kate's heart started to race.

Ellie: Answer your phone! Where are you? The guys want to go into the apartment and check things

out. I need you. I'm scared.

Ellie: Colby called the police. They're going to wait. If you don't call me soon, I'm going to start really worrying about you.

Heat filled Kate's belly. She'd told Ellie not to call the police.

Ellie: Where are you? I'm officially worried. Oh, the police are here.

Ellie: They're going in. I'm not. No way. Wish you were here to wait outside with me.

Ellie: This is Colby. Where in the heck are you? Get back here ASAP. We need you.

No more texts. Kate's heart slammed into her ribs and only short, quick breaths would come.

"Well what happened?" she murmured. She flipped over to voice messages. There were ten.

She clicked on the first one, putting it on speaker.

Sobs filled the air. Chills ran over Kate's whole body. "Kate," Ellie whimpered. "It's bad. It's really bad. The apartment is gone. Gone. I'm in an ambulance with Colby. They're taking him to the hospital. I shouldn't have let them go to the apartment. I should have made them listen." Sobs and cries. "Call me."

Kate rocked back and forth as she clicked on message after message. She felt dizzy, disoriented. Ellie's voice was barely audible and Kate had to turn up the volume and start it again. "We're at the hospital. My parents said to call your FBI guy, so I did. He's going to take care of us. Kate, it's been hours. Why haven't you called me? I told Special Agent Johansen that you were missing. I hope it isn't true and your phone just died or something. Call me, please." She sniffled before hanging up.

A jolt of hope filled Kate. Special Agent Johansen would take care of them for sure. Still, her chest ached and her stomach roiled wondering what was up with Colby.

"We're at the airport now. Please. Please be okay." Ellie sounded rushed.

"We're on the plane. Colby's going to be okay. I'm okay. The other guys are in the hospital, but everyone is going to live. Special Agent Johansen wants you to call him. I want you to call me, but they are taking our phones. Whatever you hear, know that we are safe. This is my last call. I love you, Kate. Bye."

23

Kate looked at her phone and then shook it when there were no more messages. She listened for the timestamp. Ellie's last message had been sent two hours ago. She'd barely missed them. And now it would be hours before she'd be able to talk to them. She stood and clicked on Johansen's name.

"It's Kate," she said when he picked up. Her hands shook.

"Kate. Are you okay?" The connection sounded choppy.

Relief rushed over her just hearing his voice. "Yes. What about Ellie and Colby?"

"Are you still in Italy?"

"Yes. What's going on?" She paced the room.

"We've got your family. And the Lamberts. Ellie and Colby are on their way. Now we only need you."

"My family?" Kate stopped and looked blankly out a picture window.

"Well, we've got your dad and your brothers and sisters. Your mom is another story."

Kate gasped. "Where is she? Is she okay?"

"She's fine. At least I hope she's fine."

"What?" Her stomach roiled.

"She hopped on a flight to Italy, to get you."

"You're kidding, right?" Kate grimaced. What airport was she flying into? Did the mafia know about her adoptive mom? Could they find her when she got here? Would they hurt her?

"No. I'm not kidding." His voice was flat and anger boiled beneath his words.

"Why didn't you force her to stay? It's dangerous here." She bit her lip and started pacing again.

"We can't force her to stay here. When Ellie and Colby get here, the U.S. Marshals will protect them too."

"Why though? Why are you protecting them?" A deep worry settled over Kate. What was going on?

"They are in danger because of their connection to you."

Her mouth went dry, like the Sahara Desert dry. "Me?"

"Yes."

"Why?" But Kate knew why.

"You know the answer to that."

"The mafia found my family? The Lamberts?" She gasped. There was crackling on the line.

"Let's back up. It wasn't only the apartment in Italy that was bombed. Your home and the Lamberts' went up only hours later."

"No!" Kate sat down in a leather arm chair, her hand cradling her head.

"Yes. The bombers left a note taped to the mailbox in Italy. It was signed by someone named Veronica. I'm assuming that means something to you?" So, it was Veronica who'd figured it out after all. Veronica. Had their nice Marconi driver helped her find them? Then she remembered Martino. Had he played a part in the bombing too? Panic surged and a crystal clear focus hit into her.

"Yes, she's a Marconi. She trained me in Jersey. She set up the bombing?"

"My intel on her says that's unlikely. She was most likely leaving you a nice little message, but she probably wasn't the person who set it up."

Kate couldn't make herself think about that right now. "How is everyone? I still haven't heard."

"Colby was burned, but he will be okay. One police officer was killed—the first one to enter, and everyone else has varying degrees of injuries. Ellie had a pretty bad cut on her leg from flying debris, but it's been stitched up and should heal nicely." Static interrupted his next few words. "...was remotely triggered. Looks like they waited for the light in Colby's room to go on before they set it off. You and Ellie were staying in there?"

"Yes."

"We're guessing something in there had your information on it, or part of it, which led them to your house in the States."

Kate let out a heavy breath.

"Our primary concern now is you. Specifically, how to get you back to the States safely so we can reunite you with your family."

"This is crazy. I can't. I mean..."

"You haven't told me where you are. According to Ellie, you've been kidnapped by the bad guys, but here you are talking to me. Are you safe?"

"Yes. I'm at my grandma's."

"I was unaware you had family in Italy. Did you find Carmela?"

A harsh prickling sensation rushed through her body. "I'm with my mom's mom."

"Carmela's?" Kate heard whispers as well as the tip-tapping of someone typing in the background as well as whispers.

"No. Abrie's mom. If it's any consolation, I didn't know this grandma was still around either."

"Well, I guess that explains why your mom was so determined to go to Italy. Perhaps your grandmother called her."

"Maybe," Kate said, not believing it.

"Once we get you back here, you'll be put into protective custody and get a new life."

It hit her then what he meant. She would never return to Texas. She and her family as well as the Lamberts would be on the run for the rest of their lives. Why? Because of the Marconis. Anger rose up inside her, trying to claim her. The Marconis were now playing with her future. She could hear Special Agent Johansen speaking, but she could no longer understand the words. Her anger was turning to rage. How dare they steal her life? She had to find a way to get revenge now. She wanted to blow up their homes. She wanted to destroy their lives.

She hung up without another word.

Kate pressed her back into the sofa and groaned. She needed to talk to Ellie and Colby. "How can I get revenge?" she whispered.

She sat, staring at a point on the wall until she heard the cook call everyone to lunch and ignored Johansen's persistent attempts to call her back. Kate stood like a robot, and went to the table where she sat with three large men. Two had close cropped beards and mustaches and the third was the one who had collected the horses earlier. She heard them introduce themselves, but couldn't remember any names. Her mind was elsewhere.

Kate was pulled out of her thoughts when her grandma entered the room. "Sorry I'm late, I just got some interesting news."

It occurred to Kate that her grandma had a lot of experience with the mafia. Kate could talk to her about what was going on. She'd know what to do. Kate's eyes flicked from ranch hand to ranch hand. Only then did she realize how huge they were. They were obviously more than they appeared. Maybe they could help her get revenge as well.

"Kate," her grandma said as she took a seat. "Are you okay?"

Kate shook her head. "No. No, I'm not. We need to talk."

All the men stopped eating. "Alright. Let's talk."

Once again, Kate's eyes fell on each of the men and she said, "Alone."

"They know all my business. You can speak freely here."

"Respectfully, they don't know all mine." Kate spoke in an even, low tone. Her grandma had just confirmed these men were way more important than simple ranch hands.

Her grandmother nodded and the men cleared out without a word. Even the cook, who'd been cleaning up, exited the room without protest.

"What is it?" Her grandmother pushed her plate to the center of the table.

"Colby is hurt. The apartment, my house, Ellie's house—they're all gone."

"Hold on. Start at the beginning." Her grandmother put her elbows on the table and clasped her hands together.

"The Marconis blew up Colby's place in Bologna. He barely got out alive. The blast killed a policeman and a whole bunch of other people are hurt and in the hospital." Tears came unbidden to her eyes and spilled onto her cheeks.

"How do you know it was the Marconis?" Her grandma moved to the chair next to Kate and put her arm around her.

"One of them, Veronica, left a note."

"I see."

"She saw me at a party. I hoped she wouldn't find out I wasn't supposed to be there, but she must have and now my whole family is in danger."

"I'll send someone to protect them. We'll get them out of there."

"The FBI already has. They're with the U.S. Marshals now."

Her grandma nodded and bit on her cheek. "Good," she said absently. "They destroyed your parents' home too?"

"Yeah. And Ellie's family lives only two houses away from ours. It wouldn't have been hard for them to locate her family after finding mine."

"What I need to know, Kate, is what happened between you and the Marconis to make you a target."

Kate relayed the whole story to her grandma, about finding Vinny and discovering he was a Bellini and in the mafia, and how she'd tried to save Duran, and how the Bellinis had planned to train her as an associate and groom her to be a defense attorney. And finally, how Duran brought the FBI in to save her, and the run-in at the airport, along with her escape.

While Kate spoke, her grandma nodded and said, *I see, hmm,* and *yes* a lot, but nothing else. It almost felt like a test. As if her grandma was testing her to see if she'd tell her the whole truth and nothing but—or that Kate was confirming what her grandma had already been told. "It may be a surprise to you, but..."

Just then they heard someone scream from the other room. "I'm her daughter! Get your hands off me." Her grandma stood.

Moments later, Kate's mom was being dragged, kicking and screaming into the kitchen by two massive men.

"Mom!" Kate cried and moved forward, but stopped when a guard came out of nowhere and held her back.

"We found her trying to hop the wall," the smaller of the two men said.

Abrie's scowl darkened when her eyes lit on her mother. She appeared more than ready to pick a fight.

"Let go of me," Kate said as she pulled and squirmed to get free. The man held her tight.

"It's okay," her grandma said to the guards. "Welcome home, Abrielle."

The men let go of the two of them and Kate stared at her mom, who stared right back. "Gather your things," she said to Kate. "We need to go."

24

Kate went to her mom. "Are you okay?"

"Yes, but we need to go."

Her grandmother looked again at Kate. "I told you it would be ugly."

"Is this the secret you've been keeping from me, Mom? Guess the cat's out of the bag."

Her mom sucked in a quick breath.

"Mom, please. It's okay. You're Italian and your parents are like mine. It's okay."

Her mom bristled. "I don't have any parents. They are dead." Her voice was deep, harsh.

"Come, Abrielle. As you can see, I have not been able to join your father just yet. Let's move into the family room and take a seat."

Abrie lifted her hand into the air and pointed a finger at her mom. "You had no right to take her. We are leaving."

Kate sighed, moving quickly away from her mom and into the family room. She claimed a spot on the couch once again while her grandmother sat in a chair across from Kate. They needed to hash everything out. Her mom threw her hands into the air, huffed and sat down next to Kate, glaring at Alessa the whole time.

"I just filled Grandma in on what happened to Colby and Ellie and…" Kate swallowed hard and a hiccup followed.

"Oh, sweetie." Kate's mom pulled her into a hug, rocking her like she always did when she comforted Kate. "It'll be okay. Everyone is okay. Everyone is safe. I'm so glad you are safe." Kate could feel the anger pulsing off of her mom, which was something she'd never felt before.

"It's awful, Mom. Awful."

"I know." She brushed Kate's tears from her face and kissed her forehead. "I wish I could take the hurt away."

"It's all my fault," she cried into her mom's shoulder.

Kate's grandma leaned forward at this. "No. It is not your fault. It is the Marconis who did this. They are the only ones at fault."

Her mom put her hands to her temples and shook her head. "Stop. I won't have you twist words to trick my daughter into doing as you please."

"I want to offer both families safe harbor here."

"I don't think so," Abrie spat. "We are going home and putting ourselves under the protection of the FBI and the U.S. Marshals. We do not need you."

"On the contrary. You don't think the mafia has people in the Witness Protection Program? You will be much safer here."

"I was never safe with you," Kate's mom hissed.

"Mom, stop. She saved me."

The admission did nothing to calm her mom's apparent rage. "Kate, listen, it may look to you like she is a good person. She has beautiful things, she looks familiar, but believe me, what she's involved in you don't want to be."

"Mom, I'm already involved. I'm sorry. But that's the cold, hard truth. The mafia is after me. I think Grandma has a good point. I want you guys to come here and be safe."

"We will not be safe here. They will kill you for sure, and then they will come for us and make no mistake about it, they will kill us. Period. I saw it. Over and over again as a child." Kate's mom shot daggers out of her eyes at her mom.

"Abrielle."

"It's Abrie."

"Abrie. I'm here."

Abrie's eyes bulged. "But your son is there and you support him furthering my father's terrible legacy."

"No. He is there slowly changing things, furthering your father's beautiful legacy." Her grandma's voice was deadly steady. "We never killed anyone."

"No." Her mom stood and screamed. "NO!"

Her grandmother stood too and scowled before shouting at her daughter. "We are doing good there, Abrie!"

Kate stood and put her arms out between the yelling women. "Stop it!"

She wondered, did being Italian mean you try to forgive, but find you never forget?

She really wished she could tell if her genes were affecting the decision she was going to make and if there was truly a way to know if they were.

One of her grandmother's men came rushing into the room. "*Signora.*" His voice was calm and sure, but insistent.

Her grandmother turned to the man and everyone fell silent.

"FBI Special Agent Johansen is asking for permission to enter the grounds."

Her grandmother looked at Abrie, ice in her eyes.

"Don't look at me. I had no idea he was coming." She shrugged her shoulders.

"He must have followed you here then."

"He's the Special Agent that I've been working with. I was talking to him a little over an hour ago," Kate piped in.

"Ah. He probably traced your call. It's no problem," she said to her guard. "Show him in." Then she turned to face Kate and her mom. The ice was gone. It was like her grandmother had done a one-eighty. "Let's go meet with him in the reception hall." She led the way to the grand room right off the stairs and the front foyer.

Johansen entered, flanked by two large men Kate had not seen before. Just how many of these guys did she keep on staff anyway? Behind them came another man in a suit, sandwiched between two other massive men with short cropped hair, who looked like they'd just left a special ops assignment.

Kate's grandma met him warmly. "Welcome to my home. I'm Alessa."

"Special Agent Johansen," Johansen said as he shook her hand. "This is Special Agent Murray, my partner." She shook his hand too, smiling the whole time.

The procession moved to Kate's mom, who said, "I'm surprised to see you here."

"We thought it in everyone's best interest that we come to assist you in bringing Kate home."

The agents also shook Kate's hand, firm and sharp.

"Take a seat," her grandma offered, her hand indicating a white sofa with maroon flowers to their left. Everyone sat, her grandmother taking a finely made dark leather chair and Kate and her mom sitting on a striped settee.

"I'm sorry you came all this way for me," Kate said, the sensation of doing a free-fall hitting her hard. "But, I'm not leaving. Not now anyway." She saw a spark light in her grandma's eyes, a sense of satisfaction swept over Kate. She felt strong. Important. Wise.

Her mom's head whipped to face her. "Excuse me?"

"Mom, I'm staying here for a while. Grandma will keep me safe."

"I'm your mother. You are a minor and you will do as I say. We are going with Special Agent Johansen who will turn us over to the U.S. Marshals, and they will keep us safe, together, as a family."

"I'm seventeen, almost eighteen. I am old enough to make this decision. I refuse to put our family in any more danger and I feel safe here." Kate's eyes flitted over the eight massive bodyguards surrounding the room. The sight was exactly what she needed right then.

"Kate," Special Agent Johansen said. "I think your mom is right. You should come with us. You will be safe with the Marshals, and we think you should stay with your family as long as you can."

"No."

"You have no idea who this woman is." Abrie stared at her mom. She started to say something else, but then glanced over at the FBI agents.

"I know more than you think." Kate opened her eyes wide to try to convey she knew knew about the pictures and all about her grandparents being involved with the mafia.

Alessa stood. "Well, I guess you have your answer, Special Agent Johansen."

Neither agent moved.

"Kate," Special Agent Johansen said. "I want you to really consider coming back with us where we can guarantee your safety."

"Listen. I appreciate what you're saying, but I also know that there is no guarantee. Witness Protection is not infallible. I'm safer here."

Special Agent Johansen glanced at Kate's grandma who was still standing. "I hate to be the one to inform you of this, but your grandmother here has very strong ties to the mafia, and I can't say this would be a safe environment for you."

"I know. Her son is a mafia boss." Kate said it matter-of-factly. "She, however, is here. She left that life. And truthfully, I think that makes it even safer for me to be here. She knows all the mafia's tricks and has a source there. She can keep me safe, I know it." Kate stared at her grandma who smiled.

Johansen licked his lips and narrowed his eyes.

Kate's mom leaned back hard into the sofa with a huff. "You can't trust her, Kate. She is not who she is pretending to be."

"And who exactly," her grandmothers said, "am I pretending to be?"

"Kate's benevolent protector."

"That's exactly who I intend to be. And as I mentioned earlier, you are all welcome here. Your entire family as well as the Lamberts. We have plenty of room and it would be a lot of fun to get to know everyone."

"Over my dead body," Abrie said. "And you are not keeping Kate." She stood and turned to the special agents. "Get Kate and let's go."

The body guards who had seemed to melt into the background each took a step forward. Kate's grandma held up her hand and they stopped.

"You can't force me, Mom, and if you try, I'll run. Just like you did. It's my turn now. You know as well as I do that the mafia's focus will be on getting me, not you guys. By staying here, I am helping you stay safe. That's what I want. I want our family and the Lamberts safe."

Her mom did not say a thing.

"Go, Mom. I'll be okay and when it's safe, I'll come home. I promise. We can talk all the time." She looked toward the agents and neither negated her words, which emboldened her. In truth, she knew they would not be able to be in contact. "I love you and can't wait to go back home. But now is not the time."

With tears streaming down her face, Abrie hugged Kate. "You are so stubborn. Your father is going to be beside himself with grief. He'll blame this on me."

Kate couldn't help thinking about her dad saying he thought it was a mistake not telling Kate her mom's secret and her mom saying it would be her mistake. "I think he'll understand. I'll make him understand it has nothing to do with you two."

Abrie stared at Kate for several long moments, regret and defeat in her eyes. Kate's heart twisted and a painful lump formed in her throat. Abrie sighed and then gave Alessa a death glare before turning back to Kate and saying, "Stay safe and if anything happens or you feel unsafe, call Agent Johansen and we will get you out."

Kate swallowed hard, unable to dislodge the lump. "I will. Give kisses to everyone." Her voice cracked with emotion, but she held back the tears. "Ellie—she won't understand, but hug her for me. Colby too."

She lifted her chin and looked at the ceiling to fend off the hot tears burning in her eyes.

Her mom nodded, but said nothing. Her eyes were rimmed with red and splotches assaulted her neck. Kate allowed a single tear to fall as she walked her mom to the front door, the agents and her grandmother following close behind. She stood in the door, watching as they drove away. She didn't move until they were out of sight.

Her grandmother put her arm around her. "Come inside. We have a lot to talk about."

"Tell me it has to do with revenge," Kate said, her face cold and hard.

Thank you for leaving a review!

It helps me more than you know. Big Hugs!

Pick up *Kate Unleashed (Code of Silence: Book 3)* the next book in the trilogy.

Know Cindy's news before anyone else by joining her book club http://eepurl.com/GL2HL Get sneak peaks and free stuff!

If you loved this book, try these fun novels and series:

Jump into the exciting adventures of the *Watched Trilogy*
Up the stakes and suspense with *Adrenaline Rush*
Dive in to great mystery in *Gravediggers*
Laugh and cry with Brooklyn in *Sweet and Sour Kisses*

Visit Cindy on her website:
cindymhogan.com on Google plus: Cindy M. Hogan, Instagram, and Pinterest
Follow Cindy M. Hogan on twitter: @Watched1

For series trivia, sneak peeks, events in your area, contests, fun fan interaction, like the Watched Facebook Page: Watched-the book

About the Author

Cindy M Hogan is inspired by the unpredictable teenagers she teaches. More than anything she loves the time she has with her own teenage daughters and wishes she could freeze them at this fun age. If she's not reading or writing, you'll find her snuggled up with the love of her life watching a great movie or planning their next party. Most of all, she loves to laugh.

She is the bestselling and award winning author of the *Watched trilogy*, a YA suspense series with a dash of romance. She has since branched off to write a mystery, *Gravediggers*, that won Best YA novel of 2013, a contemporary romance, *Sweet and Sour Kisses*, and *The Code of Silence Trilogy*. She also has written three novellas: *Dangerous Truth*, *The Descension*, and *The Royal Guard*.

To learn more about the author and all the books she has written, visit her at cindymhogan.com

www.ingramcontent.com/pod-product-compliance
Lightning Source LLC
Chambersburg PA
CBHW070114030726
47506CB00002B/742